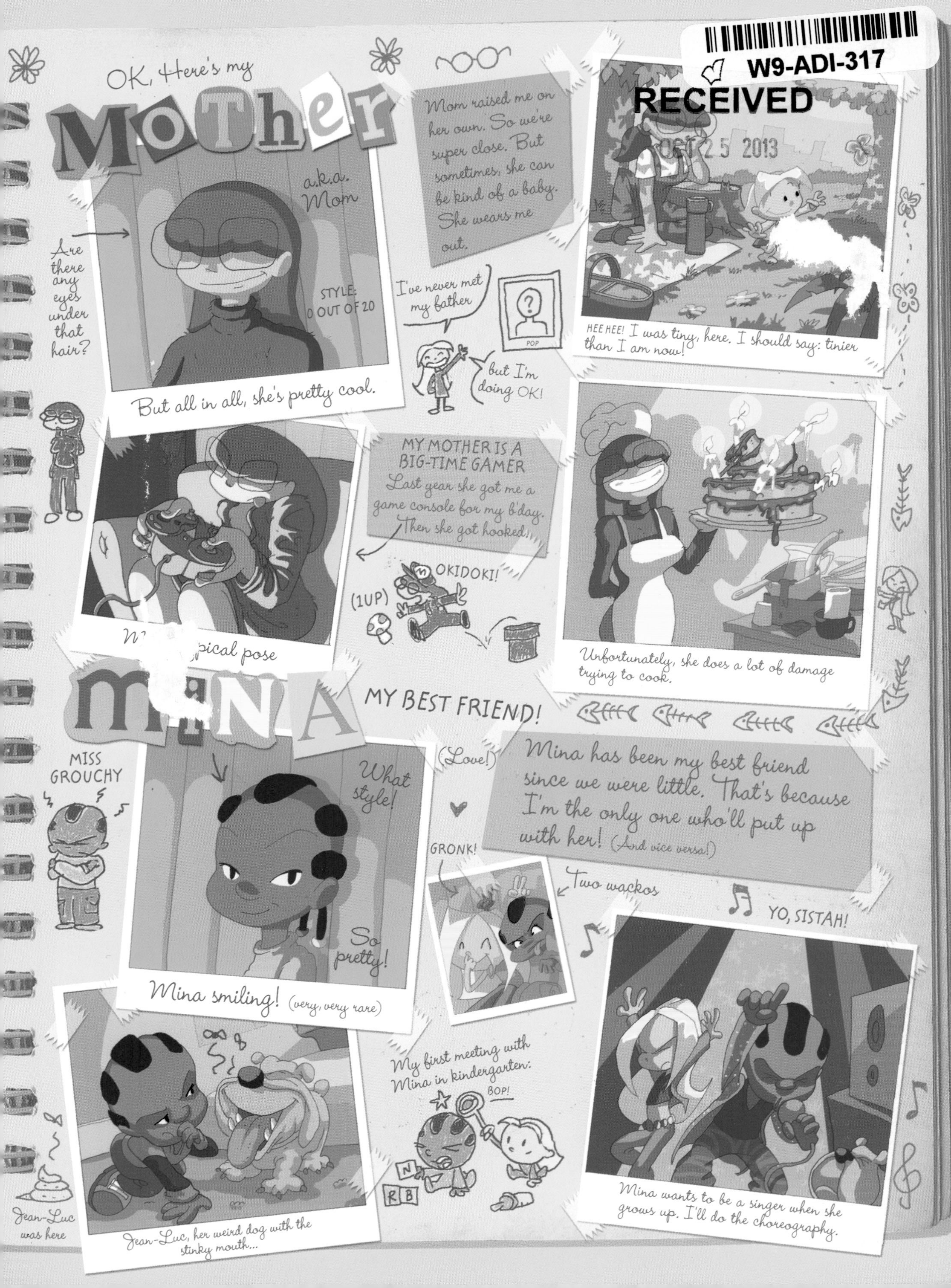
OK, Here's my
MOTher
a.k.a. Mom
Are there any eyes under that hair?
STYLE: 0 OUT OF 20
But all in all, she's pretty cool.
Mom raised me on her own. So we're super close. But sometimes, she can be kind of a baby. She wears me out.
I've never met my father
POP
but I'm doing OK!
HEE HEE! I was tiny, here. I should say: tinier than I am now!
MY MOTHER IS A BIG-TIME GAMER
Last year she got me a game console for my b'day. Then she got hooked.
OKIDOKI!
(1UP)
pical pose
Unfortunately, she does a lot of damage trying to cook.
MY BEST FRIEND!
MISS GROUCHY
What style!
So pretty!
Mina smiling! (very, very rare)
(Love!)
Mina has been my best friend since we were little. That's because I'm the only one who'll put up with her! (And vice versa!)
GRONK!
Two wackos
YO, SISTAH!
My first meeting with Mina in kindergarten:
BOP!
N
R B
Jean-Luc was here
Jean-Luc, her weird dog with the stinky mouth...
Mina wants to be a singer when she grows up. I'll do the choreography.

LOU! 1

Secret Diary

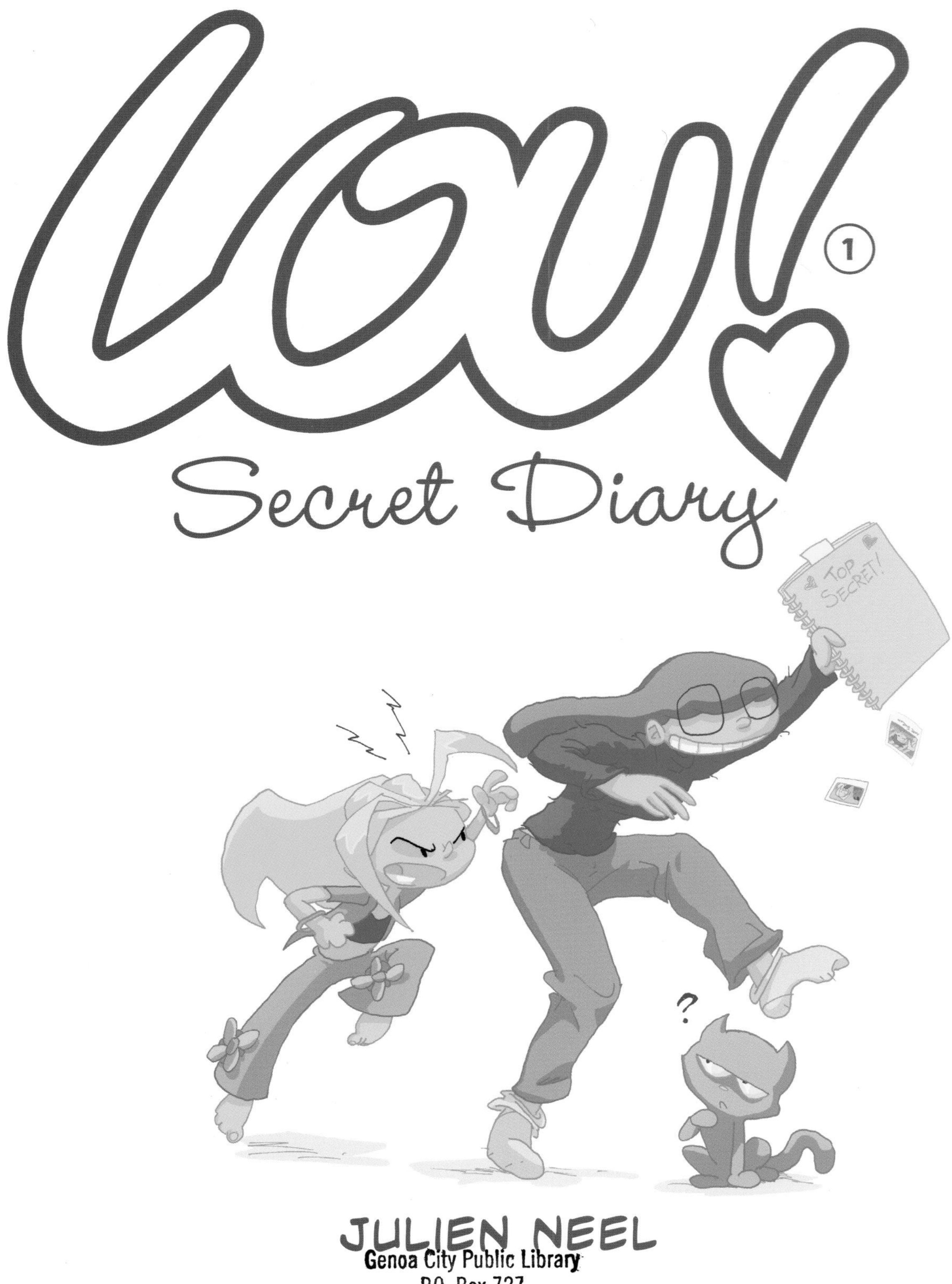
TOP SECRET!
?

JULIEN NEEL

GRAPHIC UNIVERSE™ · MINNEAPOLIS · NEW YORK

TO CAROLE AND MAÏA

Story and art by Julien Neel

Translation by Carol Klio Burrell

First American edition published in 2012 by Graphic Universe™.

Lou! by Julien Neel © 2004 — Glénat Editions
© 2012 Lerner Publishing Group, Inc. for the US edition

Graphic Universe™ is a trademark of Lerner Publishing Group, Inc.

Graphic Universe™
A division of Lerner Publishing Group, Inc.
241 First Avenue North
Minneapolis, MN 55401 U.S.A.

Website address: www.lernerbooks.com

Library of Congress Cataloging-in-Publication Data

Neel, Julien.
  Secret diary / story and art by Julien Neel ; translation by Carol Klio Burrell.
       p.   cm. —— (Lou! ; #1)
  Summary: Lou shares the high and low points of being twelve as she takes a few awkward steps into dating, plays matchmaker for her single mother, and discovers, along with her best friend Mina, that they may be outgrowing playing with dolls.
  ISBN: 978-0-7613-8776-3 (lib. bdg. : alk. paper) 1. Graphic novels [1. Graphic novels 2. Mothers and daughters——Fiction. 3. Dating (Social customs)——Fiction.] I. Burrell, Carol Klio. II. Title.
  PZ7.7.N44Se 2012
  741.5'973——dc23   2011026432

Manufactured in the United States of America
1 – BC – 12/31/11

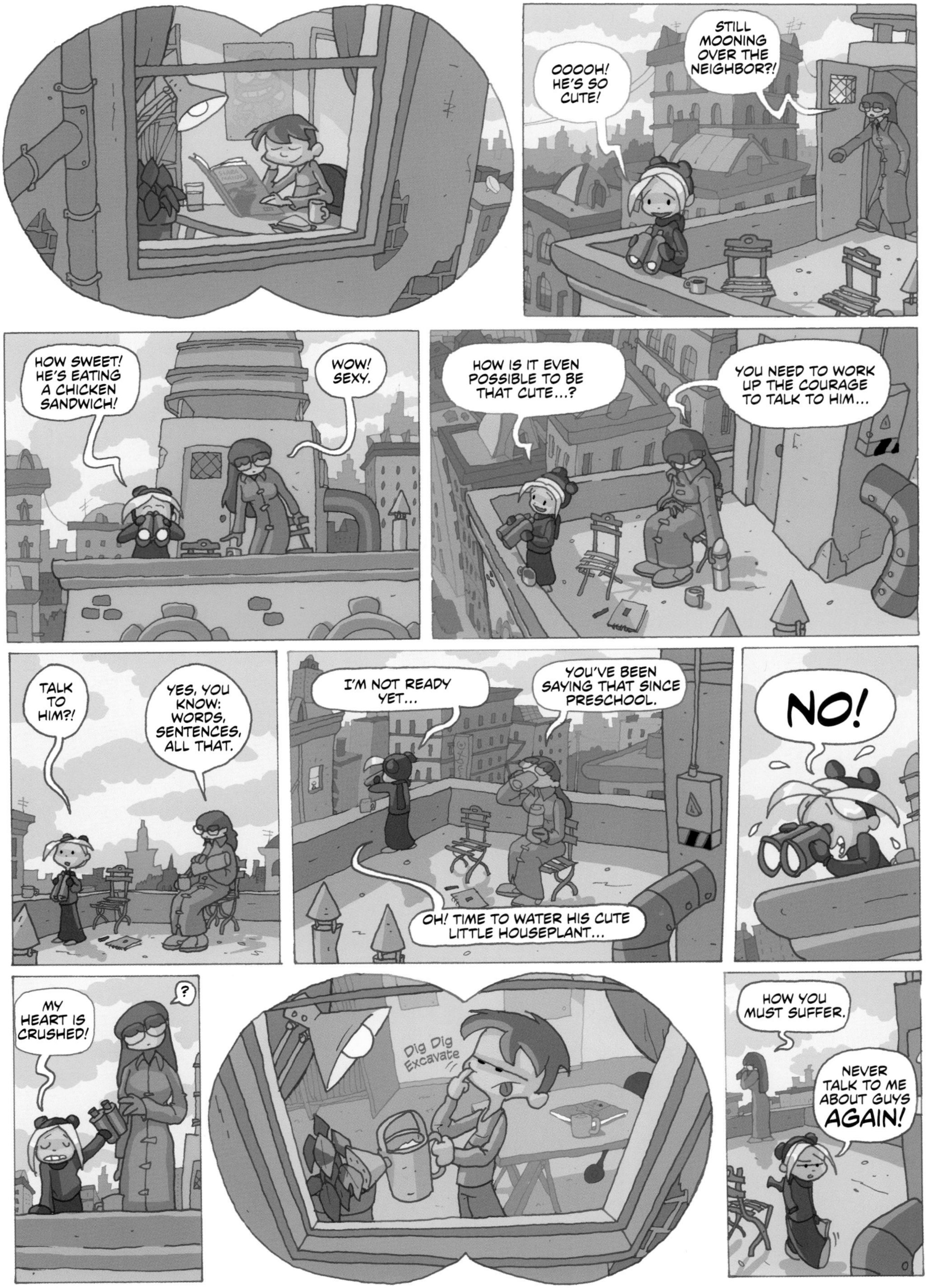

OOOOH! HE'S SO CUTE!
STILL MOONING OVER THE NEIGHBOR?!
HOW SWEET! HE'S EATING A CHICKEN SANDWICH!
WOW! SEXY.
HOW IS IT EVEN POSSIBLE TO BE THAT CUTE...?
YOU NEED TO WORK UP THE COURAGE TO TALK TO HIM...
TALK TO HIM?!
YES, YOU KNOW: WORDS, SENTENCES, ALL THAT.
I'M NOT READY YET...
YOU'VE BEEN SAYING THAT SINCE PRESCHOOL.
OH! TIME TO WATER HIS CUTE LITTLE HOUSEPLANT...
NO!
MY HEART IS CRUSHED!
?
Dig Dig Excavate
HOW YOU MUST SUFFER.
NEVER TALK TO ME ABOUT GUYS AGAIN!

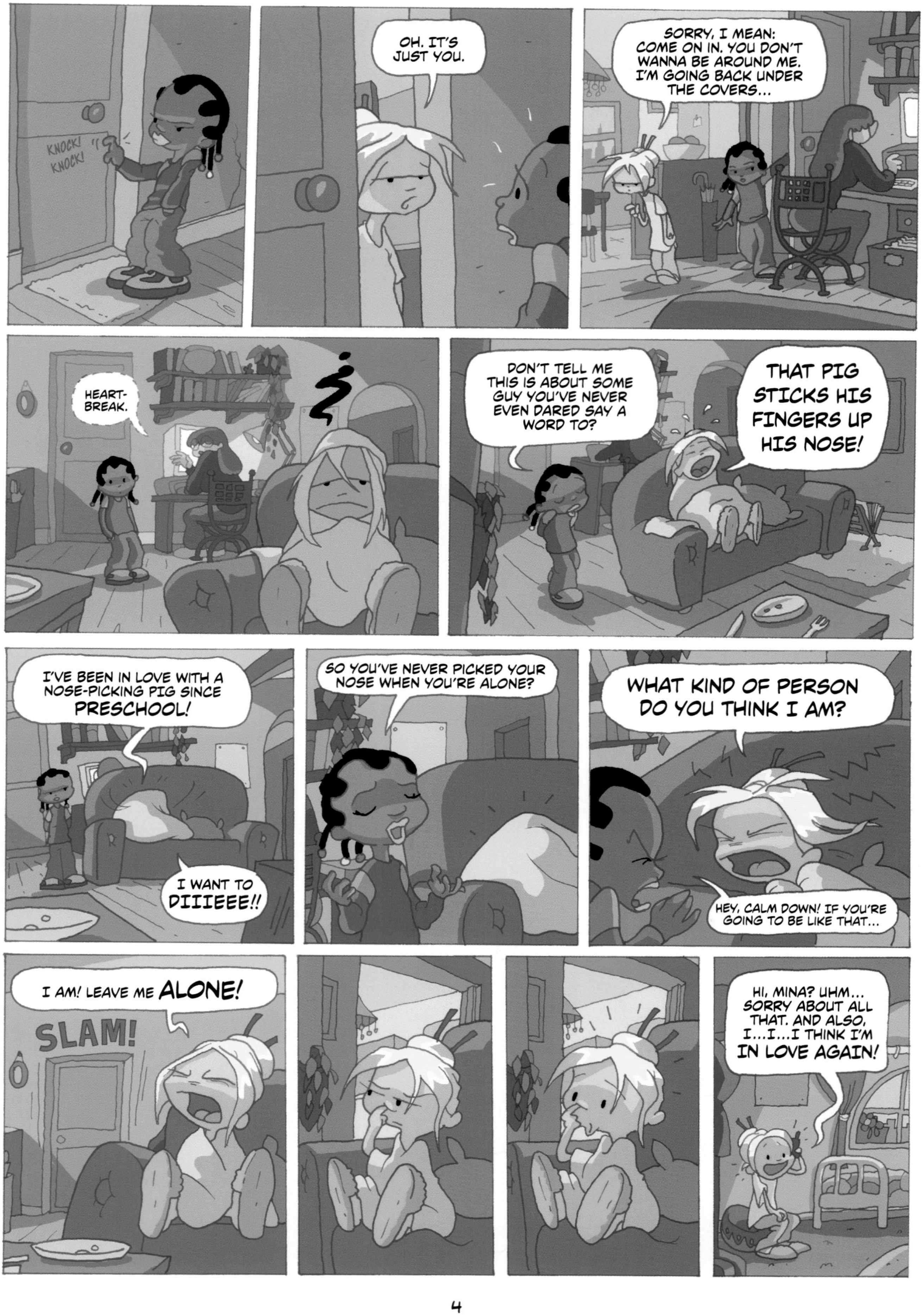
KNOCK! KNOCK!
OH. IT'S JUST YOU.
SORRY, I MEAN: COME ON IN. YOU DON'T WANNA BE AROUND ME. I'M GOING BACK UNDER THE COVERS...
HEART-BREAK.
DON'T TELL ME THIS IS ABOUT SOME GUY YOU'VE NEVER EVEN DARED SAY A WORD TO?
THAT PIG STICKS HIS FINGERS UP HIS NOSE!
I'VE BEEN IN LOVE WITH A NOSE-PICKING PIG SINCE PRESCHOOL!
I WANT TO DIIIEEE!!
SO YOU'VE NEVER PICKED YOUR NOSE WHEN YOU'RE ALONE?
WHAT KIND OF PERSON DO YOU THINK I AM?
HEY, CALM DOWN! IF YOU'RE GOING TO BE LIKE THAT...
I AM! LEAVE ME ALONE!
SLAM!
HI, MINA? UHM... SORRY ABOUT ALL THAT. AND ALSO, I...I...I THINK I'M IN LOVE AGAIN!

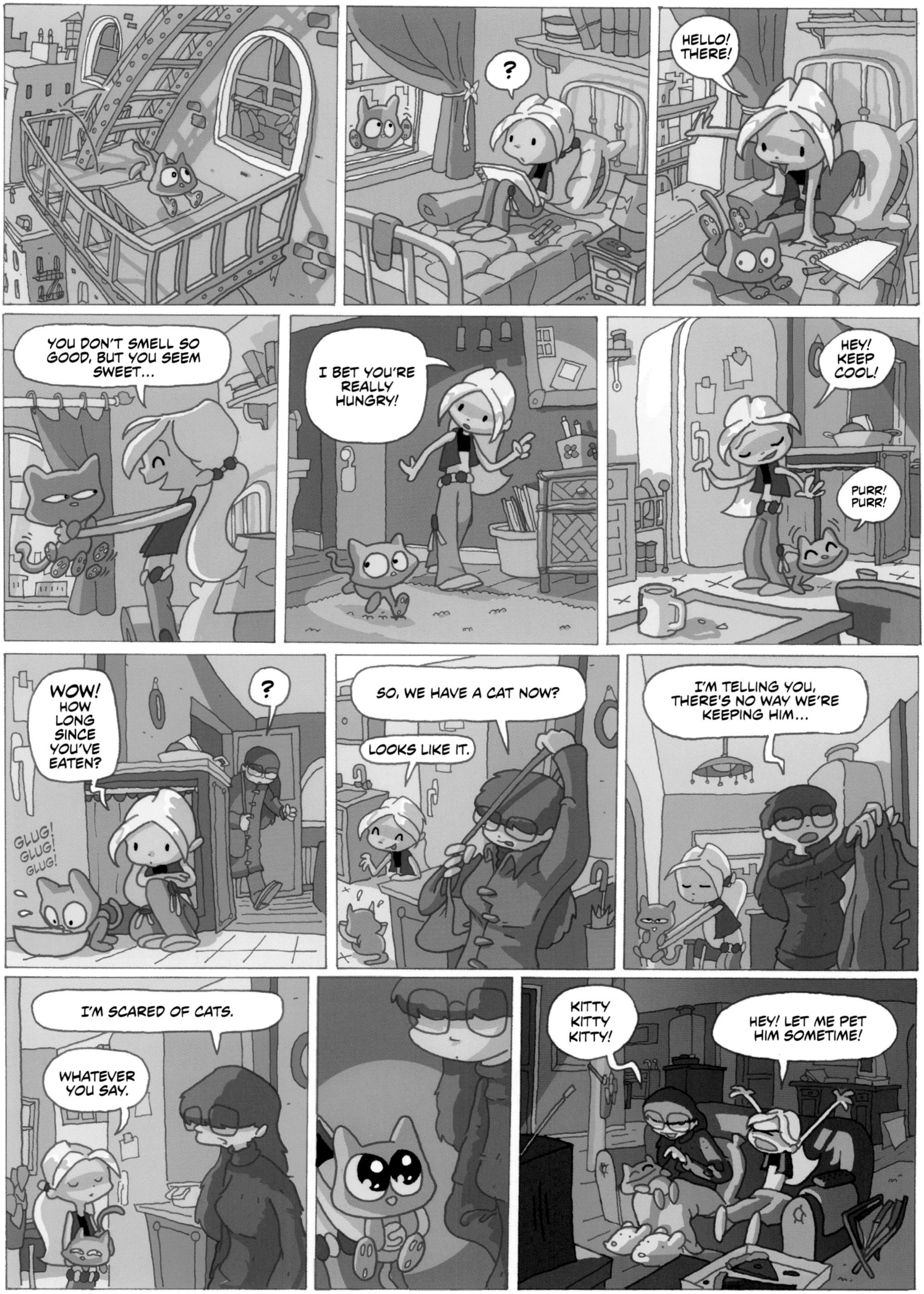
?
HELLO! THERE!
YOU DON'T SMELL SO GOOD, BUT YOU SEEM SWEET...
I BET YOU'RE REALLY HUNGRY!
HEY! KEEP COOL!
PURR! PURR!
WOW! HOW LONG SINCE YOU'VE EATEN?
GLUG! GLUG! GLUG!
?
SO, WE HAVE A CAT NOW?
LOOKS LIKE IT.
I'M TELLING YOU, THERE'S NO WAY WE'RE KEEPING HIM...
I'M SCARED OF CATS.
WHATEVER YOU SAY.
KITTY KITTY KITTY!
HEY! LET ME PET HIM SOMETIME!

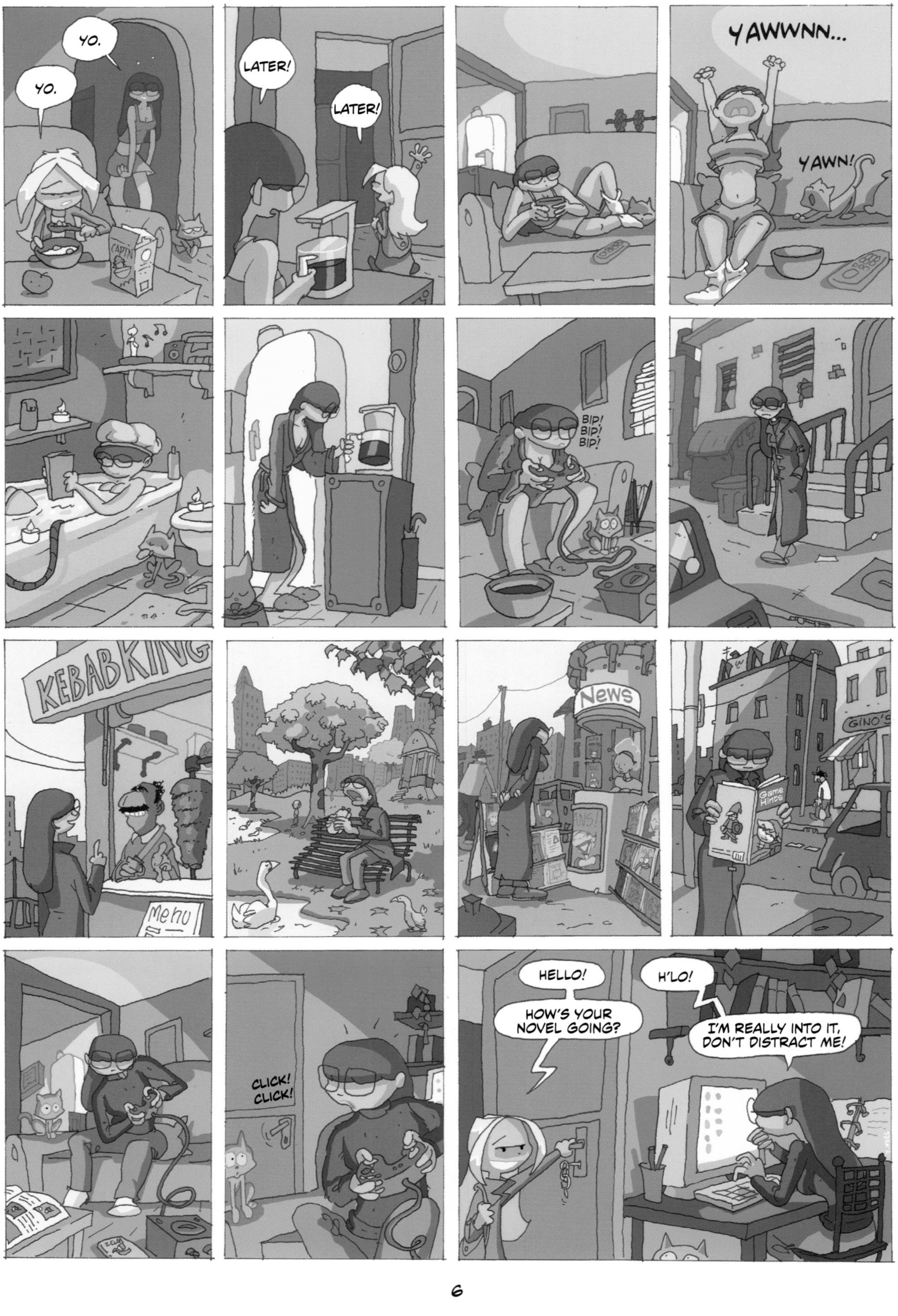
YO.
YO.
LATER!
LATER!
YAWWNN...
YAWN!
BIP! BIP! BIP!
KEBAB KING
Menu
News
GINO'S
Game Hints
CLICK! CLICK!
HELLO!
HOW'S YOUR NOVEL GOING?
H'LO!
I'M REALLY INTO IT, DON'T DISTRACT ME!

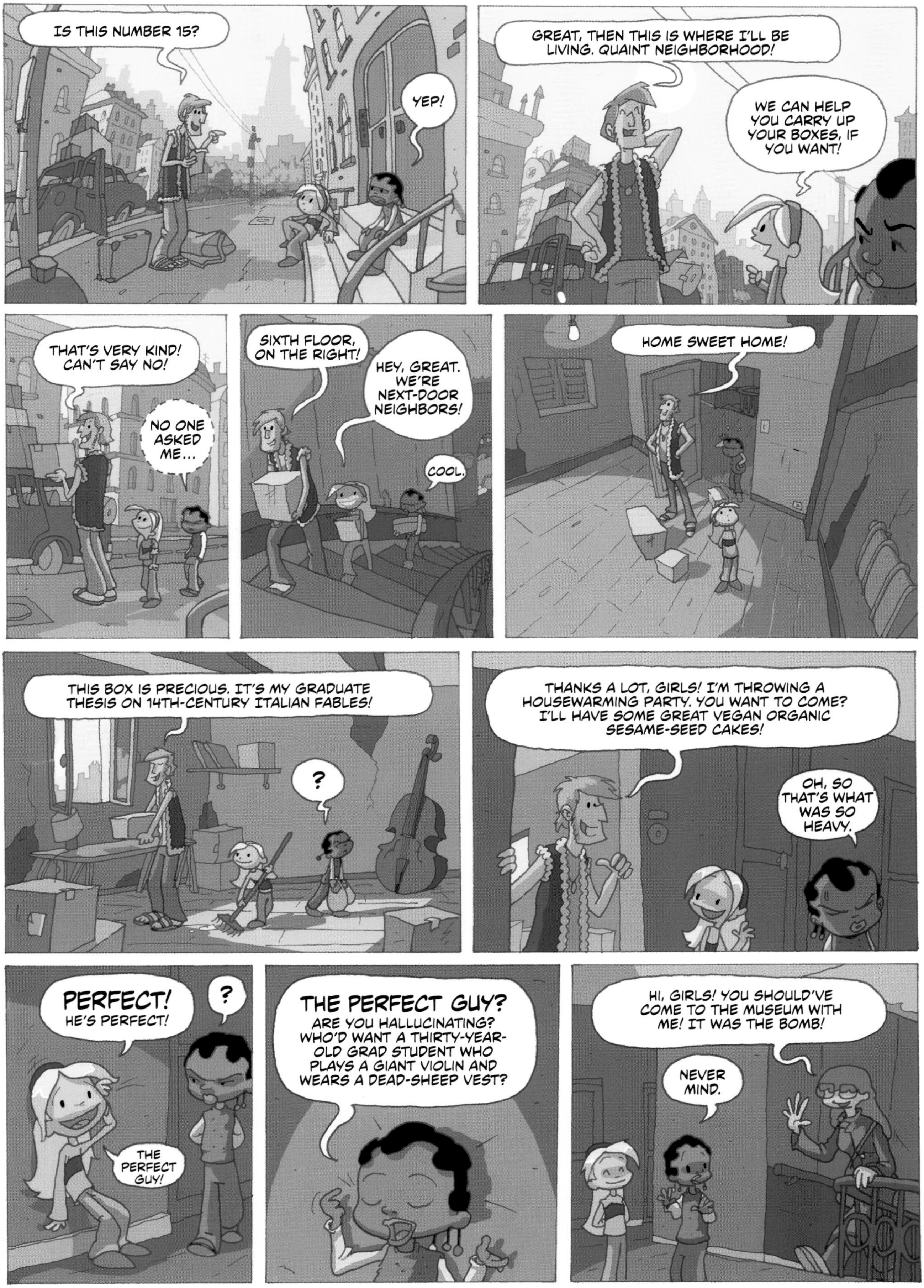
IS THIS NUMBER 15?
YEP!
GREAT, THEN THIS IS WHERE I'LL BE LIVING. QUAINT NEIGHBORHOOD!
WE CAN HELP YOU CARRY UP YOUR BOXES, IF YOU WANT!
THAT'S VERY KIND! CAN'T SAY NO!
NO ONE ASKED ME...
SIXTH FLOOR, ON THE RIGHT!
HEY, GREAT. WE'RE NEXT-DOOR NEIGHBORS!
COOL.
HOME SWEET HOME!
THIS BOX IS PRECIOUS. IT'S MY GRADUATE THESIS ON 14TH-CENTURY ITALIAN FABLES!
?
THANKS A LOT, GIRLS! I'M THROWING A HOUSEWARMING PARTY. YOU WANT TO COME? I'LL HAVE SOME GREAT VEGAN ORGANIC SESAME-SEED CAKES!
OH, SO THAT'S WHAT WAS SO HEAVY.
PERFECT! HE'S PERFECT!
?
THE PERFECT GUY!
THE PERFECT GUY? ARE YOU HALLUCINATING? WHO'D WANT A THIRTY-YEAR-OLD GRAD STUDENT WHO PLAYS A GIANT VIOLIN AND WEARS A DEAD-SHEEP VEST?
HI, GIRLS! YOU SHOULD'VE COME TO THE MUSEUM WITH ME! IT WAS THE BOMB!
NEVER MIND.

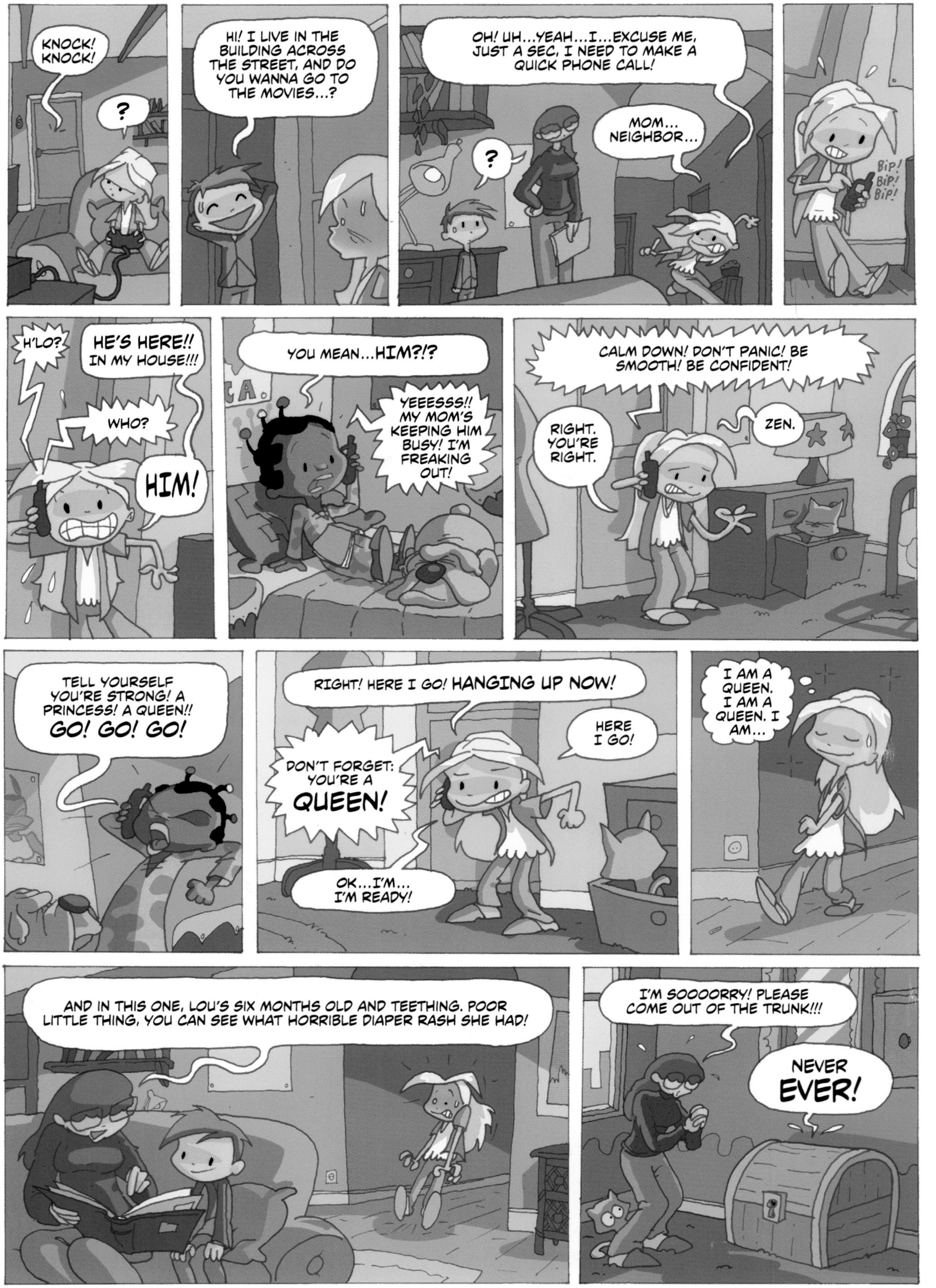
KNOCK! KNOCK!
?
HI! I LIVE IN THE BUILDING ACROSS THE STREET, AND DO YOU WANNA GO TO THE MOVIES...?
OH! UH...YEAH...I...EXCUSE ME, JUST A SEC, I NEED TO MAKE A QUICK PHONE CALL!
?
MOM... NEIGHBOR...
BIP! BIP! BIP!
H'LO?
HE'S HERE!! IN MY HOUSE!!!
WHO?
HIM!
YOU MEAN...HIM?!?
YEEESSS!! MY MOM'S KEEPING HIM BUSY! I'M FREAKING OUT!
CALM DOWN! DON'T PANIC! BE SMOOTH! BE CONFIDENT!
RIGHT. YOU'RE RIGHT.
ZEN.
TELL YOURSELF YOU'RE STRONG! A PRINCESS! A QUEEN!! GO! GO! GO!
RIGHT! HERE I GO! HANGING UP NOW!
HERE I GO!
DON'T FORGET: YOU'RE A QUEEN!
OK...I'M... I'M READY!
I AM A QUEEN. I AM A QUEEN. I AM...
AND IN THIS ONE, LOU'S SIX MONTHS OLD AND TEETHING. POOR LITTLE THING, YOU CAN SEE WHAT HORRIBLE DIAPER RASH SHE HAD!
I'M SOOOORRY! PLEASE COME OUT OF THE TRUNK!!!
NEVER EVER!

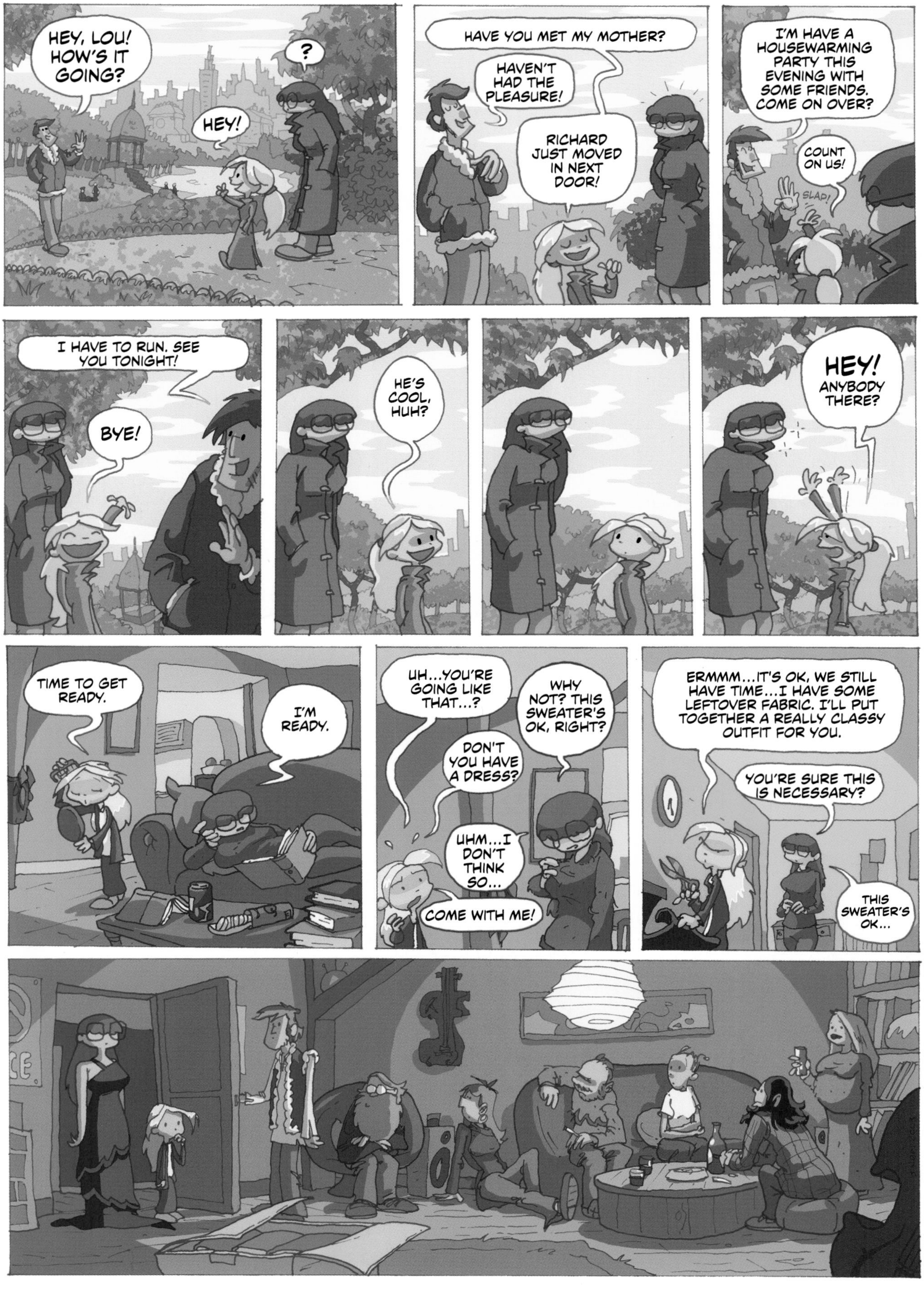
HEY, LOU! HOW'S IT GOING?
?
HEY!
HAVE YOU MET MY MOTHER?
HAVEN'T HAD THE PLEASURE!
RICHARD JUST MOVED IN NEXT DOOR!
I'M HAVE A HOUSEWARMING PARTY THIS EVENING WITH SOME FRIENDS. COME ON OVER?
COUNT ON US!
SLAP!
I HAVE TO RUN. SEE YOU TONIGHT!
BYE!
HE'S COOL, HUH?
HEY! ANYBODY THERE?
TIME TO GET READY.
I'M READY.
UH...YOU'RE GOING LIKE THAT...?
WHY NOT? THIS SWEATER'S OK, RIGHT?
DON'T YOU HAVE A DRESS?
UHM...I DON'T THINK SO...
COME WITH ME!
ERMMM...IT'S OK, WE STILL HAVE TIME...I HAVE SOME LEFTOVER FABRIC. I'LL PUT TOGETHER A REALLY CLASSY OUTFIT FOR YOU.
YOU'RE SURE THIS IS NECESSARY?
THIS SWEATER'S OK...

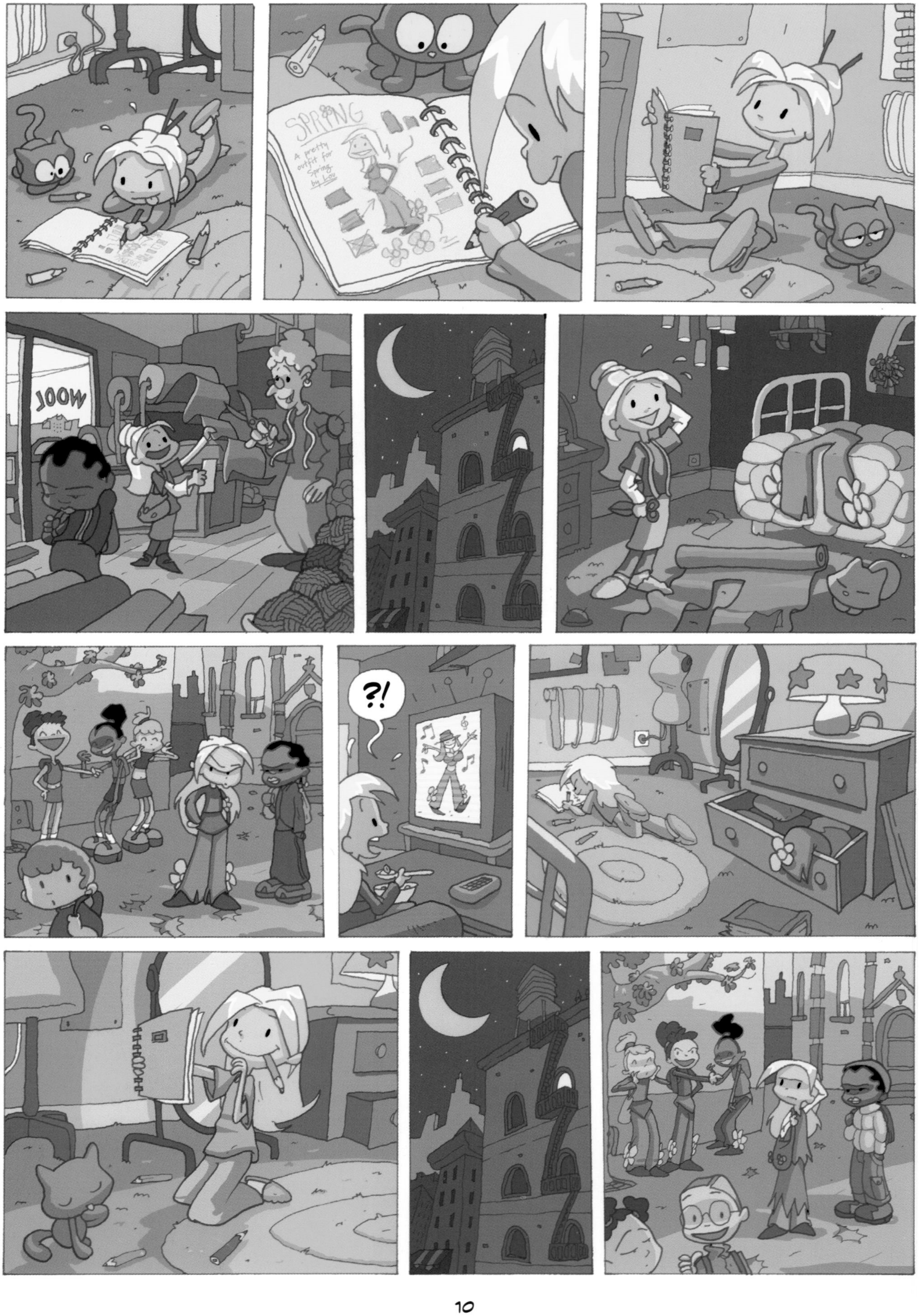
SPRING
A pretty outfit for Spring by Lou
?!

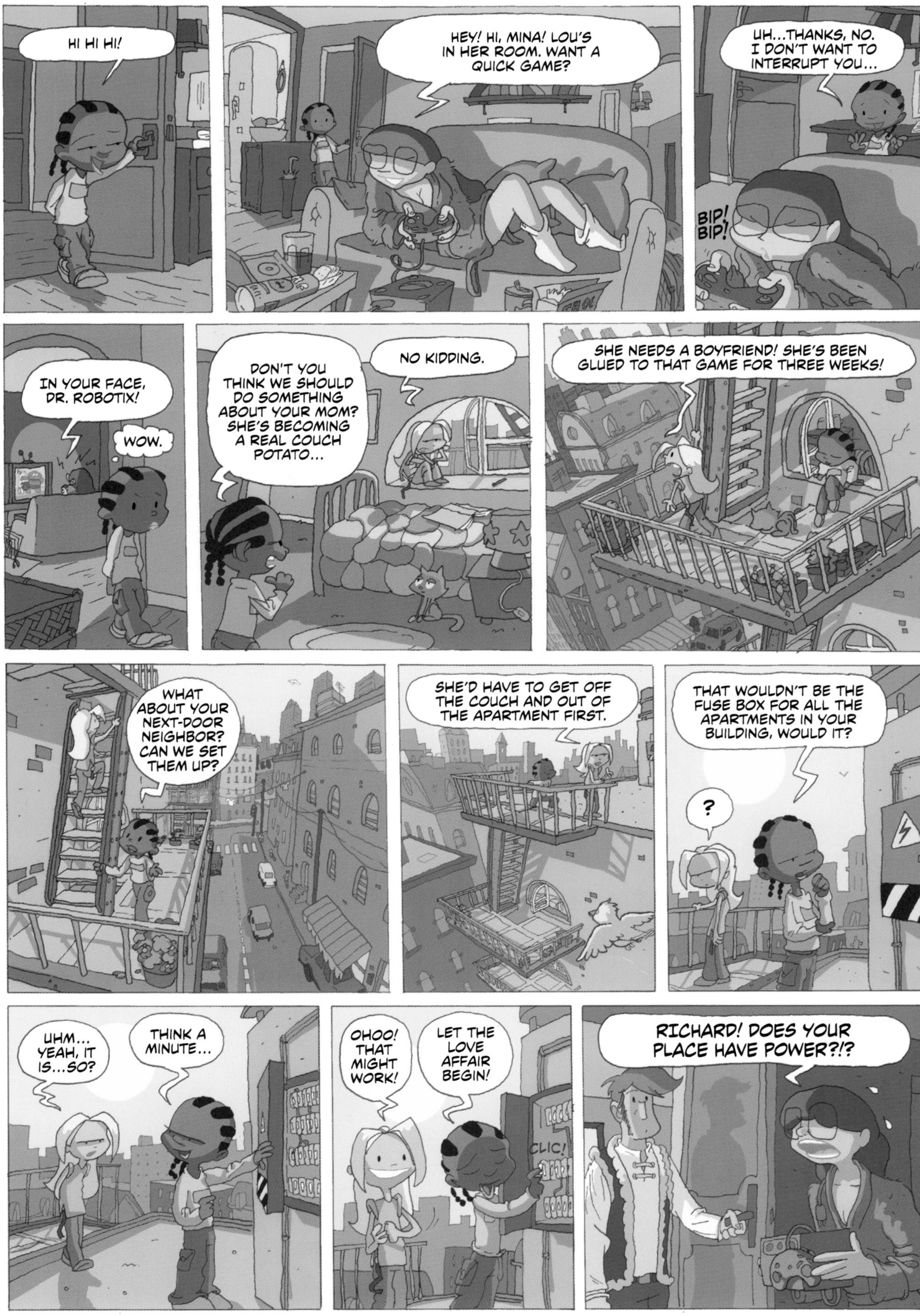
HI HI HI!
HEY! HI, MINA! LOU'S IN HER ROOM. WANT A QUICK GAME?
UH...THANKS, NO. I DON'T WANT TO INTERRUPT YOU...
BIP! BIP!
IN YOUR FACE, DR. ROBOTIX!
WOW.
DON'T YOU THINK WE SHOULD DO SOMETHING ABOUT YOUR MOM? SHE'S BECOMING A REAL COUCH POTATO...
NO KIDDING.
SHE NEEDS A BOYFRIEND! SHE'S BEEN GLUED TO THAT GAME FOR THREE WEEKS!
WHAT ABOUT YOUR NEXT-DOOR NEIGHBOR? CAN WE SET THEM UP?
SHE'D HAVE TO GET OFF THE COUCH AND OUT OF THE APARTMENT FIRST.
THAT WOULDN'T BE THE FUSE BOX FOR ALL THE APARTMENTS IN YOUR BUILDING, WOULD IT?
?
UHM... YEAH, IT IS...SO?
THINK A MINUTE...
OHOO! THAT MIGHT WORK!
LET THE LOVE AFFAIR BEGIN!
CLIC!
RICHARD! DOES YOUR PLACE HAVE POWER?!?

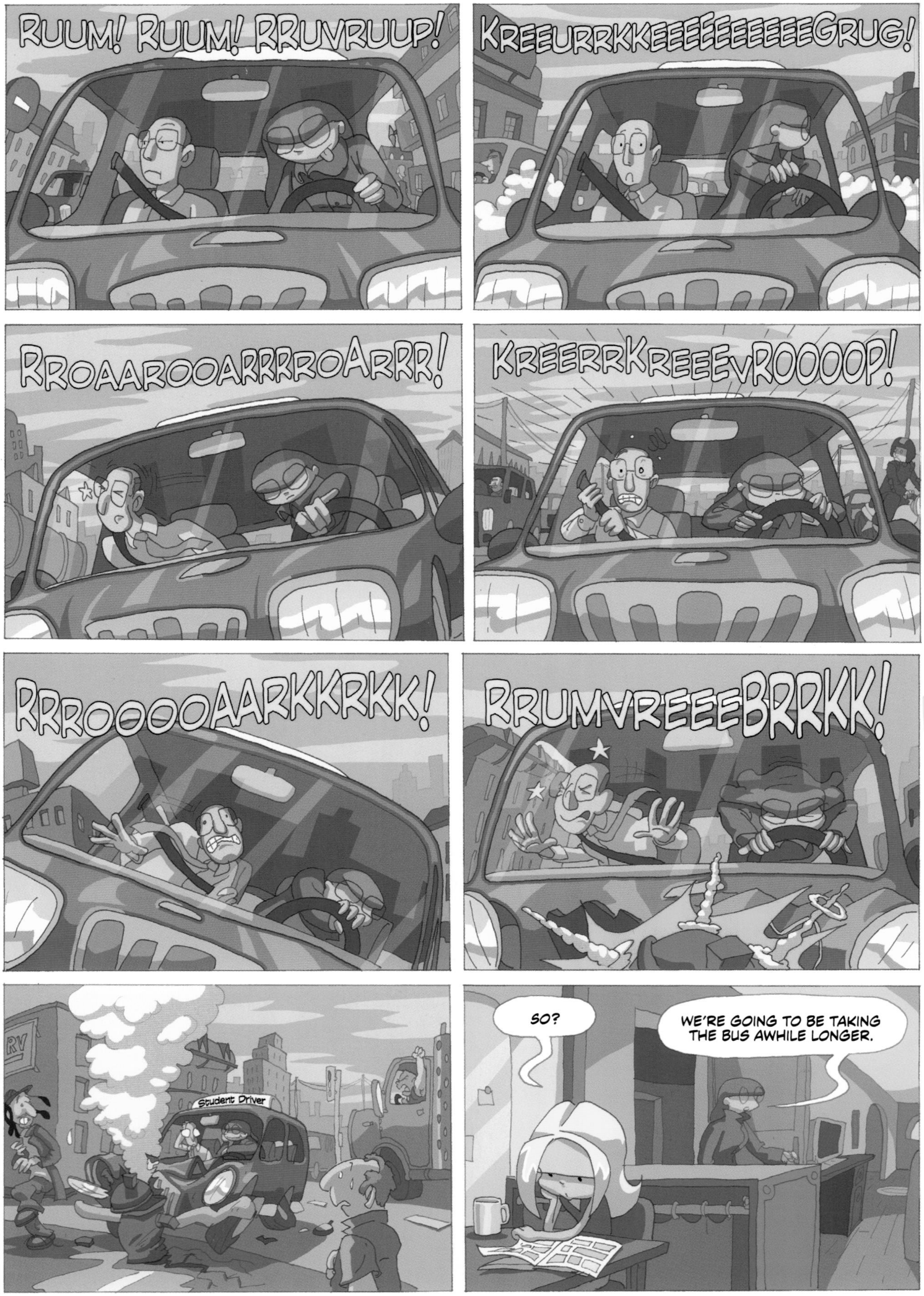

RUUM! RUUM! RRUVRUUP!
KREEURRKKEEEEEEEEEEGRUG!
RROAAROOARRRROARRR!
KREERRKREEEVROOOOP!
RRROOOOOAARKKRKK!
RRUMVREEEEBRRKK!
Student Driver
SO?
WE'RE GOING TO BE TAKING THE BUS AWHILE LONGER.

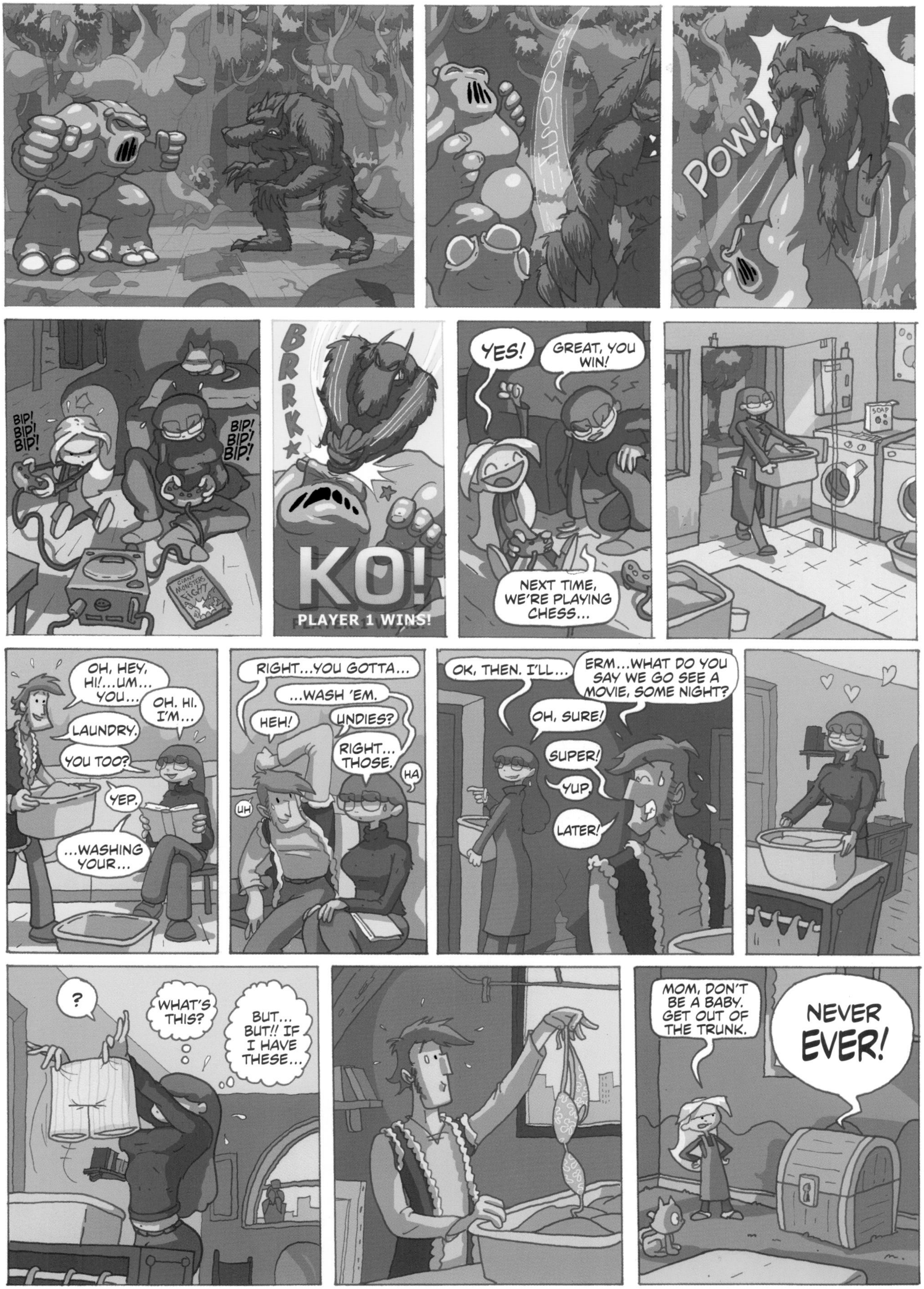
WHOOOOSH!
POW!
BIP! BIP! BIP!
BIP! BIP! BIP!
GIANT MONSTERS FIGHT
BRRK
KO!
PLAYER 1 WINS!
YES!
GREAT, YOU WIN!
NEXT TIME, WE'RE PLAYING CHESS...
SOAP
OH, HEY, HI!...UM... YOU...
OH. HI. I'M...
LAUNDRY.
YOU TOO?
YEP.
...WASHING YOUR...
RIGHT...YOU GOTTA...
...WASH 'EM.
HEH!
UNDIES?
RIGHT... THOSE.
HA
UH
OK, THEN. I'LL...
ERM...WHAT DO YOU SAY WE GO SEE A MOVIE, SOME NIGHT?
OH, SURE!
SUPER!
YUP.
LATER!
?
WHAT'S THIS?
BUT... BUT!! IF I HAVE THESE...
MOM, DON'T BE A BABY. GET OUT OF THE TRUNK.
NEVER EVER!

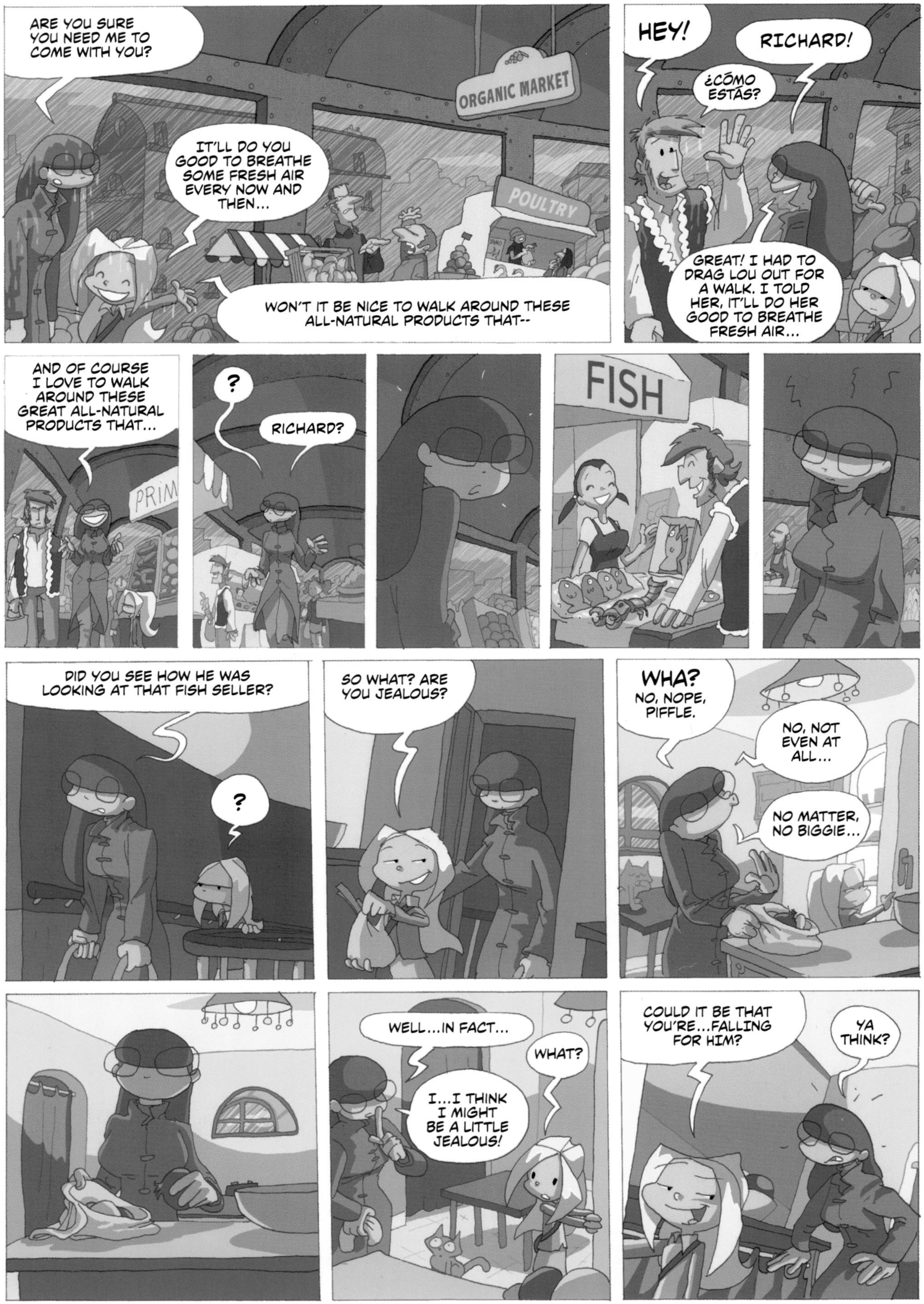
ARE YOU SURE YOU NEED ME TO COME WITH YOU?
ORGANIC MARKET
IT'LL DO YOU GOOD TO BREATHE SOME FRESH AIR EVERY NOW AND THEN...
POULTRY
WON'T IT BE NICE TO WALK AROUND THESE ALL-NATURAL PRODUCTS THAT--
HEY!
¿CÓMO ESTÁS?
RICHARD!
GREAT! I HAD TO DRAG LOU OUT FOR A WALK. I TOLD HER, IT'LL DO HER GOOD TO BREATHE FRESH AIR...
AND OF COURSE I LOVE TO WALK AROUND THESE GREAT ALL-NATURAL PRODUCTS THAT...
PRIM
?
RICHARD?
FISH
DID YOU SEE HOW HE WAS LOOKING AT THAT FISH SELLER?
?
SO WHAT? ARE YOU JEALOUS?
WHA? NO, NOPE, PIFFLE.
NO, NOT EVEN AT ALL...
NO MATTER, NO BIGGIE...
WELL...IN FACT...
WHAT?
I...I THINK I MIGHT BE A LITTLE JEALOUS!
COULD IT BE THAT YOU'RE...FALLING FOR HIM?
YA THINK?

Sidera, Cosmic Warrioress, came to a landing on the planet Oceanus, on which the insidious Neptuna was holding Prince Falgor captive...

No sooner had Sidera entered the coral fortress than a battalion of the sorceress' lobstermen attacked from all sides...

Well-versed in the arts of galactic combat, Sidera vanquished the guards and entered the lair where the terrible fish-woman had imprisoned the prince.

But Neptuna, through a cunning and underhanded magic spell, disarmed the valiant defender of galactic justice...

"This time you're finished, Sidera! The prince is in my power!" snickered the enchantress.

Quick as a flash, Sidera slammed the wicked creature with a powerful high kick to the jaw.

"That'll teach you, hussy!" retorted our heroine to the sorceress from the abyss, who lay sprawled on the ground showing everyone her disgusting, cellulite-filled thighs.

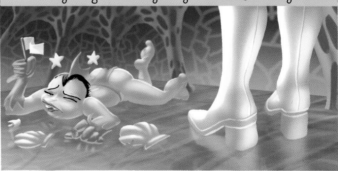

"Never fear, your highness! I have come to rescue you from the clutches of that sorceress!" announced the shapely warrior woman, breaking the prisoner's chains.

"Sidera, you have saved my life," murmured the prince. "How can I ever repay you?"

"That's easy," responded the space Amazon, placing a passionate kiss on his lips."

SO, HOW'S YOUR NOVEL GOING?

TIP TIP

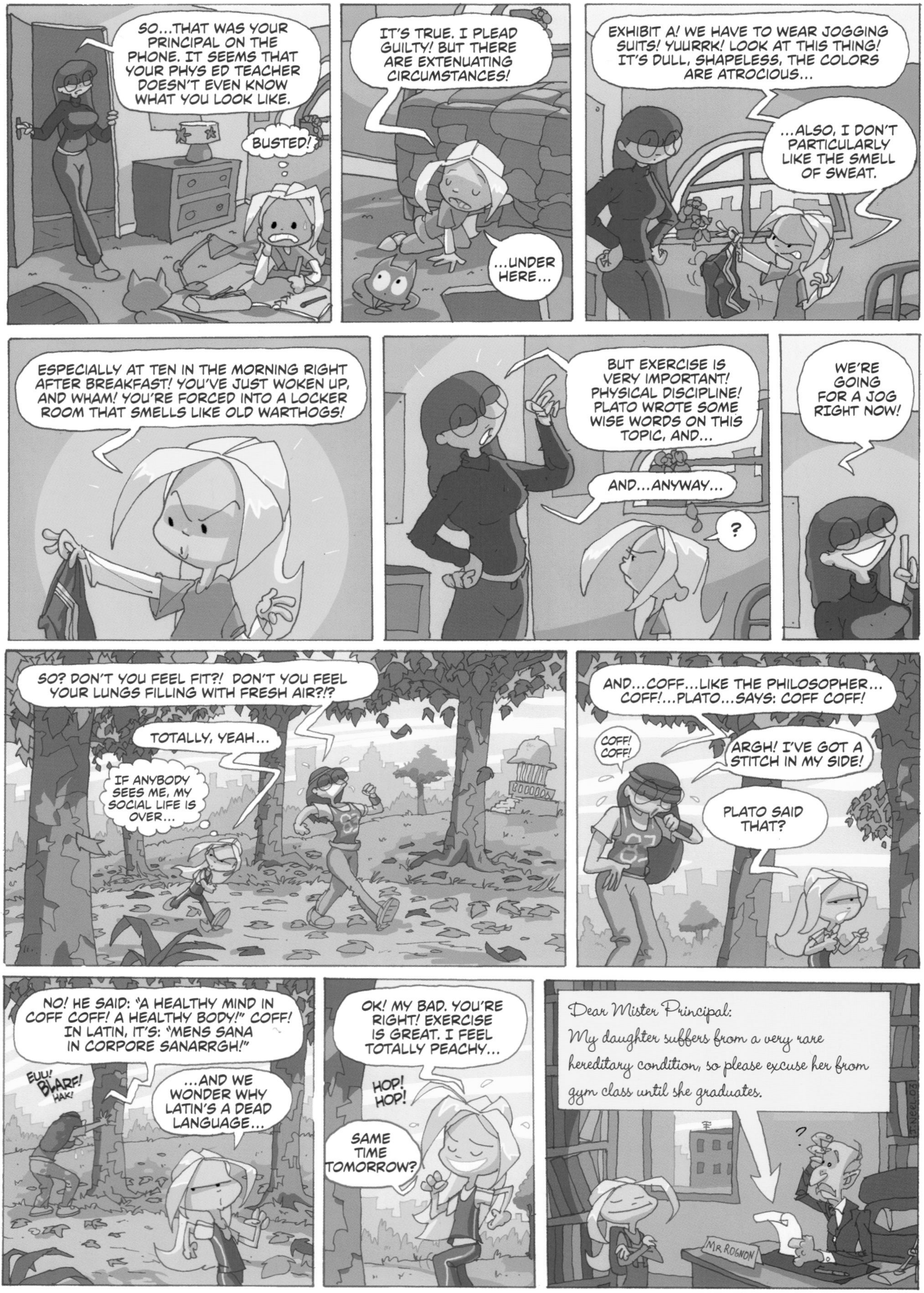
SO...THAT WAS YOUR PRINCIPAL ON THE PHONE. IT SEEMS THAT YOUR PHYS ED TEACHER DOESN'T EVEN KNOW WHAT YOU LOOK LIKE.
BUSTED!
IT'S TRUE. I PLEAD GUILTY! BUT THERE ARE EXTENUATING CIRCUMSTANCES!
...UNDER HERE...
EXHIBIT A! WE HAVE TO WEAR JOGGING SUITS! YUURRK! LOOK AT THIS THING! IT'S DULL, SHAPELESS, THE COLORS ARE ATROCIOUS...
...ALSO, I DON'T PARTICULARLY LIKE THE SMELL OF SWEAT.
ESPECIALLY AT TEN IN THE MORNING RIGHT AFTER BREAKFAST! YOU'VE JUST WOKEN UP, AND WHAM! YOU'RE FORCED INTO A LOCKER ROOM THAT SMELLS LIKE OLD WARTHOGS!
BUT EXERCISE IS VERY IMPORTANT! PHYSICAL DISCIPLINE! PLATO WROTE SOME WISE WORDS ON THIS TOPIC, AND...
AND...ANYWAY...
?
WE'RE GOING FOR A JOG RIGHT NOW!
SO? DON'T YOU FEEL FIT?! DON'T YOU FEEL YOUR LUNGS FILLING WITH FRESH AIR?!?
TOTALLY, YEAH...
IF ANYBODY SEES ME, MY SOCIAL LIFE IS OVER...
AND...COFF...LIKE THE PHILOSOPHER... COFF!...PLATO...SAYS: COFF COFF!
COFF! COFF!
ARGH! I'VE GOT A STITCH IN MY SIDE!
PLATO SAID THAT?
NO! HE SAID: "A HEALTHY MIND IN COFF COFF! A HEALTHY BODY!" COFF! IN LATIN, IT'S: "MENS SANA IN CORPORE SANARRGH!"
EUU! BLARF! HAK!
...AND WE WONDER WHY LATIN'S A DEAD LANGUAGE...
OK! MY BAD. YOU'RE RIGHT! EXERCISE IS GREAT. I FEEL TOTALLY PEACHY...
HOP! HOP!
SAME TIME TOMORROW?
Dear Mister Principal:
My daughter suffers from a very rare hereditary condition, so please excuse her from gym class until she graduates.
?
MR ROGNON

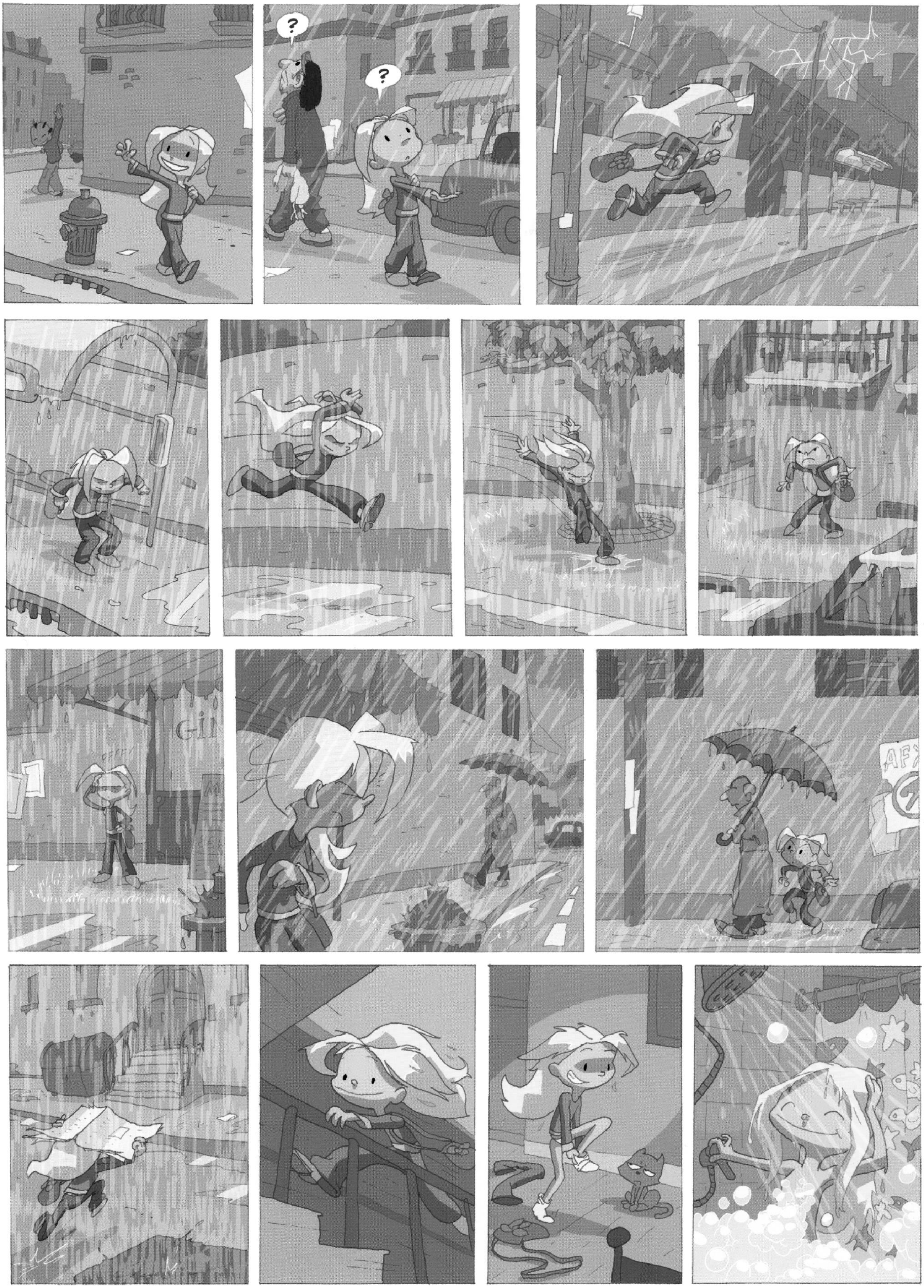
?
?

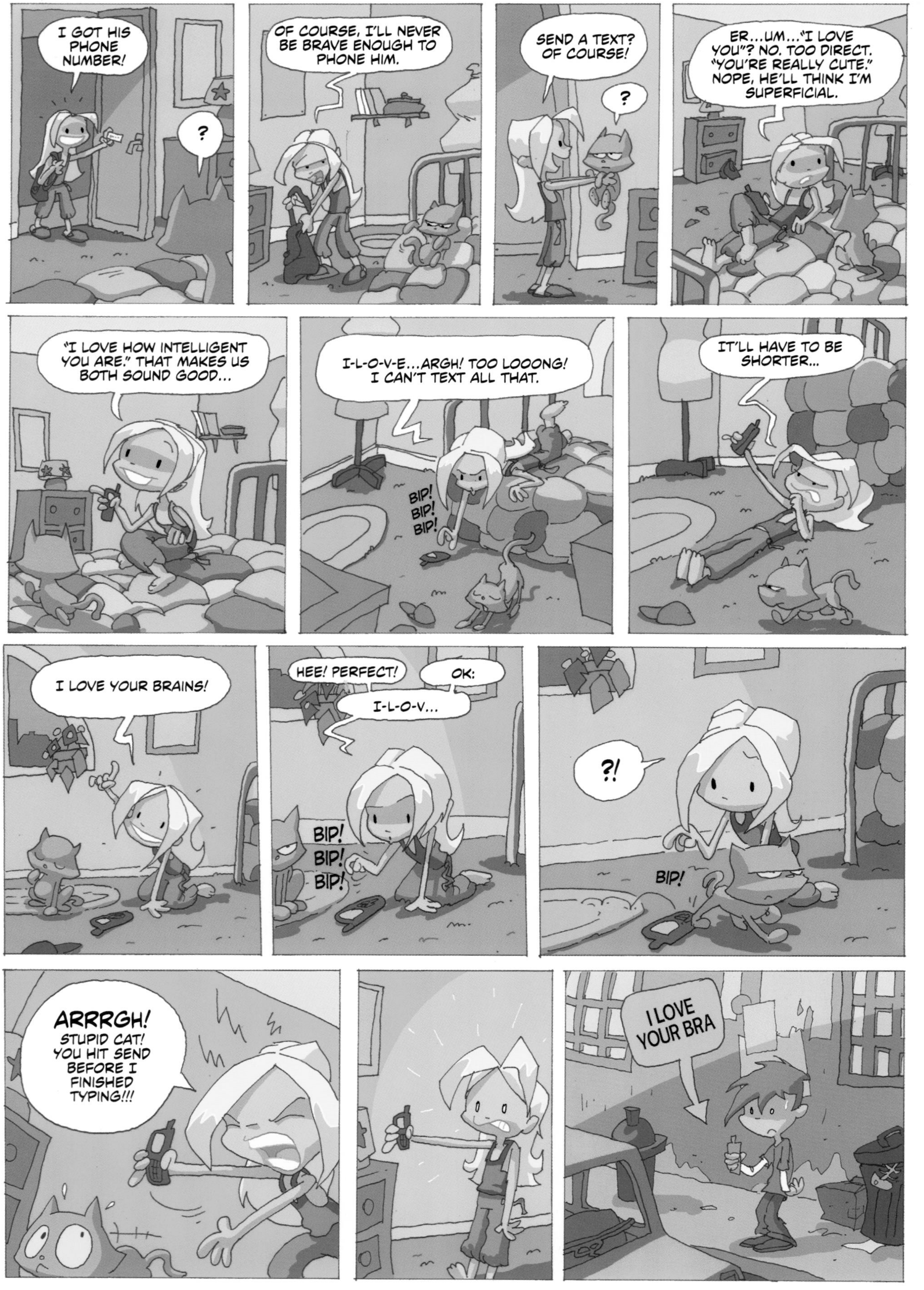
I GOT HIS PHONE NUMBER!
?
OF COURSE, I'LL NEVER BE BRAVE ENOUGH TO PHONE HIM.
SEND A TEXT? OF COURSE!
?
ER...UM..."I LOVE YOU"? NO. TOO DIRECT. "YOU'RE REALLY CUTE." NOPE, HE'LL THINK I'M SUPERFICIAL.
"I LOVE HOW INTELLIGENT YOU ARE." THAT MAKES US BOTH SOUND GOOD...
I-L-O-V-E...ARGH! TOO LOOONG! I CAN'T TEXT ALL THAT.
BIP! BIP! BIP!
IT'LL HAVE TO BE SHORTER...
I LOVE YOUR BRAINS!
HEE! PERFECT!
OK:
I-L-O-V...
BIP! BIP! BIP!
?!
BIP!
ARRRGH! STUPID CAT! YOU HIT SEND BEFORE I FINISHED TYPING!!!
I LOVE YOUR BRA

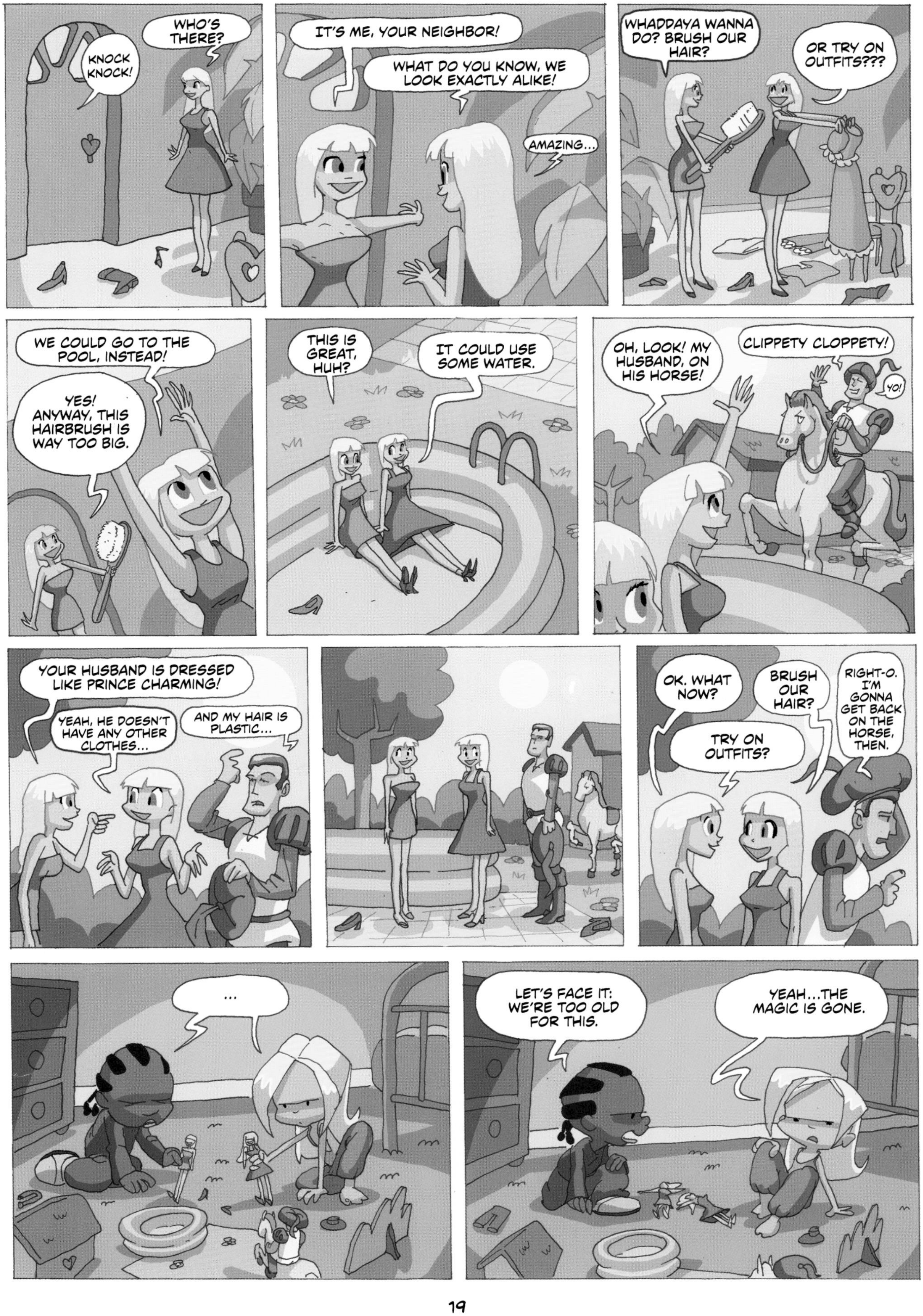
KNOCK KNOCK!
WHO'S THERE?
IT'S ME, YOUR NEIGHBOR!
WHAT DO YOU KNOW, WE LOOK EXACTLY ALIKE!
AMAZING...
WHADDAYA WANNA DO? BRUSH OUR HAIR?
OR TRY ON OUTFITS???
WE COULD GO TO THE POOL, INSTEAD!
YES! ANYWAY, THIS HAIRBRUSH IS WAY TOO BIG.
THIS IS GREAT, HUH?
IT COULD USE SOME WATER.
OH, LOOK! MY HUSBAND, ON HIS HORSE!
CLIPPETY CLOPPETY!
YO!
YOUR HUSBAND IS DRESSED LIKE PRINCE CHARMING!
YEAH, HE DOESN'T HAVE ANY OTHER CLOTHES...
AND MY HAIR IS PLASTIC...
OK. WHAT NOW?
BRUSH OUR HAIR?
TRY ON OUTFITS?
RIGHT-O. I'M GONNA GET BACK ON THE HORSE, THEN.
...
LET'S FACE IT: WE'RE TOO OLD FOR THIS.
YEAH...THE MAGIC IS GONE.

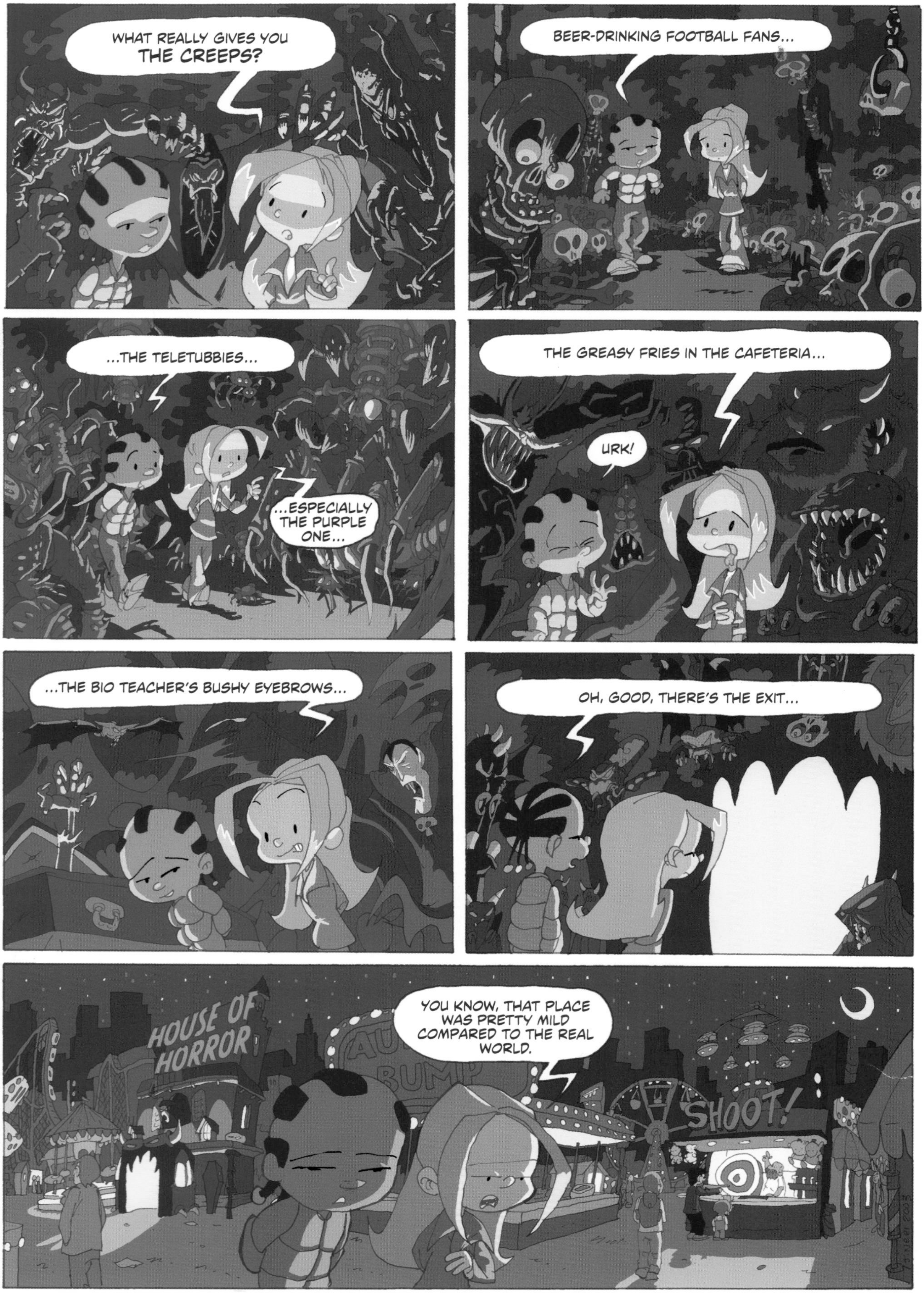
WHAT REALLY GIVES YOU THE CREEPS?
BEER-DRINKING FOOTBALL FANS...
...THE TELETUBBIES...
...ESPECIALLY THE PURPLE ONE...
THE GREASY FRIES IN THE CAFETERIA...
URK!
...THE BIO TEACHER'S BUSHY EYEBROWS...
OH, GOOD, THERE'S THE EXIT...
HOUSE OF HORROR
YOU KNOW, THAT PLACE WAS PRETTY MILD COMPARED TO THE REAL WORLD.
BUMP
SHOOT!

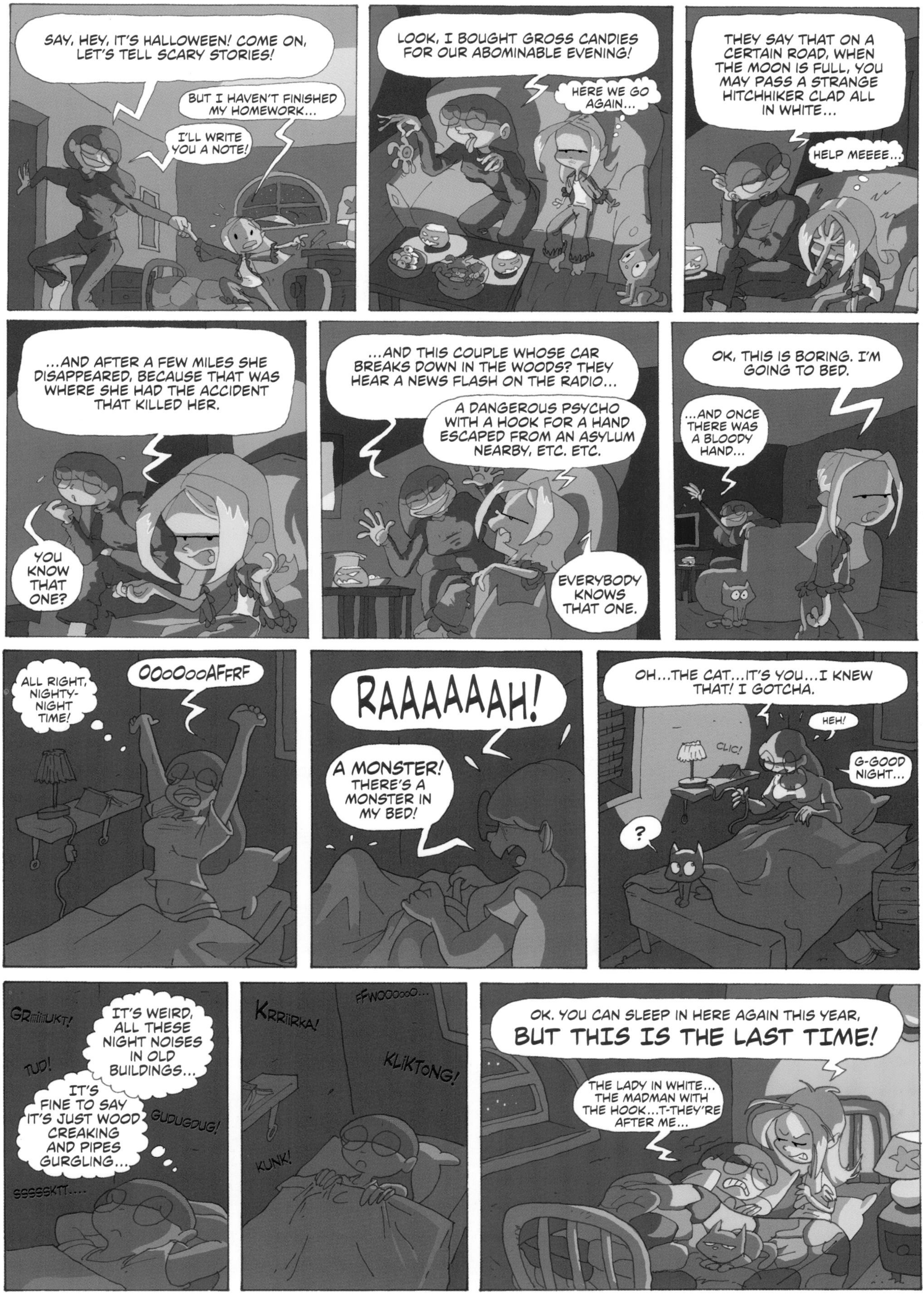
SAY, HEY, IT'S HALLOWEEN! COME ON, LET'S TELL SCARY STORIES!
BUT I HAVEN'T FINISHED MY HOMEWORK...
I'LL WRITE YOU A NOTE!
LOOK, I BOUGHT GROSS CANDIES FOR OUR ABOMINABLE EVENING!
HERE WE GO AGAIN...
THEY SAY THAT ON A CERTAIN ROAD, WHEN THE MOON IS FULL, YOU MAY PASS A STRANGE HITCHHIKER CLAD ALL IN WHITE...
HELP MEEEE...
...AND AFTER A FEW MILES SHE DISAPPEARED, BECAUSE THAT WAS WHERE SHE HAD THE ACCIDENT THAT KILLED HER.
YOU KNOW THAT ONE?
...AND THIS COUPLE WHOSE CAR BREAKS DOWN IN THE WOODS? THEY HEAR A NEWS FLASH ON THE RADIO...
A DANGEROUS PSYCHO WITH A HOOK FOR A HAND ESCAPED FROM AN ASYLUM NEARBY, ETC. ETC.
EVERYBODY KNOWS THAT ONE.
OK, THIS IS BORING. I'M GOING TO BED.
...AND ONCE THERE WAS A BLOODY HAND...
ALL RIGHT, NIGHTY-NIGHT TIME!
OOOOOOAFFRF
RAAAAAAH!
A MONSTER! THERE'S A MONSTER IN MY BED!
OH...THE CAT...IT'S YOU...I KNEW THAT! I GOTCHA.
HEH!
CLIC!
G-GOOD NIGHT...
?
GRIIIIIUKT!
IT'S WEIRD, ALL THESE NIGHT NOISES IN OLD BUILDINGS...
TUD!
IT'S FINE TO SAY IT'S JUST WOOD CREAKING AND PIPES GURGLING...
GUDUGDUG!
SSSSSSKTT....
FFWOOOOOO...
KRRIIRKA!
KLIKTONG!
KUNK!
OK. YOU CAN SLEEP IN HERE AGAIN THIS YEAR, BUT THIS IS THE LAST TIME!
THE LADY IN WHITE... THE MADMAN WITH THE HOOK...T-THEY'RE AFTER ME...

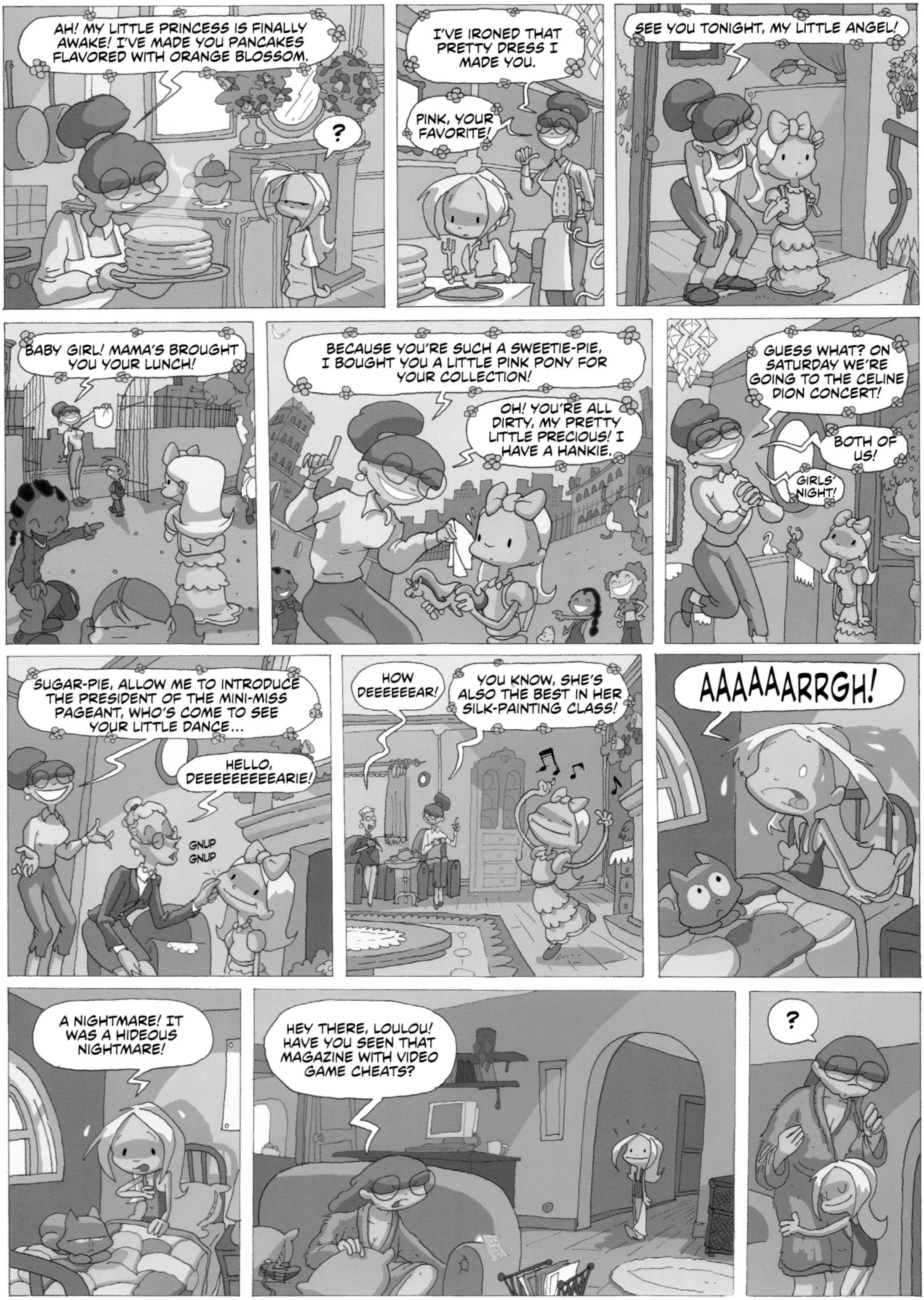
AH! MY LITTLE PRINCESS IS FINALLY AWAKE! I'VE MADE YOU PANCAKES FLAVORED WITH ORANGE BLOSSOM.
?
I'VE IRONED THAT PRETTY DRESS I MADE YOU.
PINK, YOUR FAVORITE!
SEE YOU TONIGHT, MY LITTLE ANGEL!
BABY GIRL! MAMA'S BROUGHT YOU YOUR LUNCH!
BECAUSE YOU'RE SUCH A SWEETIE-PIE, I BOUGHT YOU A LITTLE PINK PONY FOR YOUR COLLECTION!
OH! YOU'RE ALL DIRTY, MY PRETTY LITTLE PRECIOUS! I HAVE A HANKIE.
GUESS WHAT? ON SATURDAY WE'RE GOING TO THE CELINE DION CONCERT!
BOTH OF US!
GIRLS' NIGHT!
SUGAR-PIE, ALLOW ME TO INTRODUCE THE PRESIDENT OF THE MINI-MISS PAGEANT, WHO'S COME TO SEE YOUR LITTLE DANCE...
HELLO, DEEEEEEEEEARIE!
GNUP GNUP
HOW DEEEEEEAR!
YOU KNOW, SHE'S ALSO THE BEST IN HER SILK-PAINTING CLASS!
AAAAAARRGH!
A NIGHTMARE! IT WAS A HIDEOUS NIGHTMARE!
HEY THERE, LOULOU! HAVE YOU SEEN THAT MAGAZINE WITH VIDEO GAME CHEATS?
?

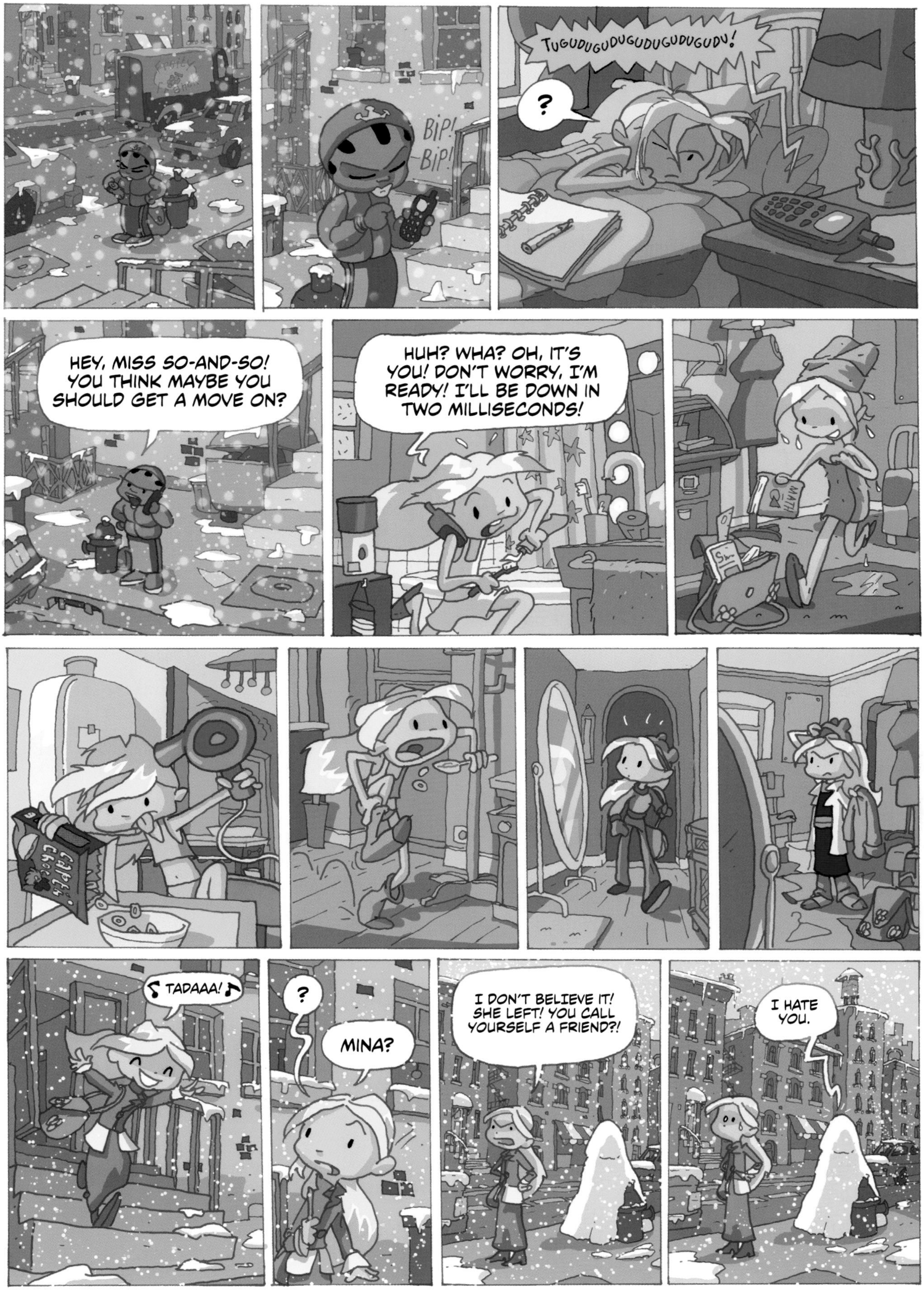
BIP! BIP!
TUGUDUGUDUGUDUGUDUGUDU!
?
HEY, MISS SO-AND-SO! YOU THINK MAYBE YOU SHOULD GET A MOVE ON?
HUH? WHA? OH, IT'S YOU! DON'T WORRY, I'M READY! I'LL BE DOWN IN TWO MILLISECONDS!
MATH
TADAAA!
?
MINA?
I DON'T BELIEVE IT! SHE LEFT! YOU CALL YOURSELF A FRIEND?!
I HATE YOU.

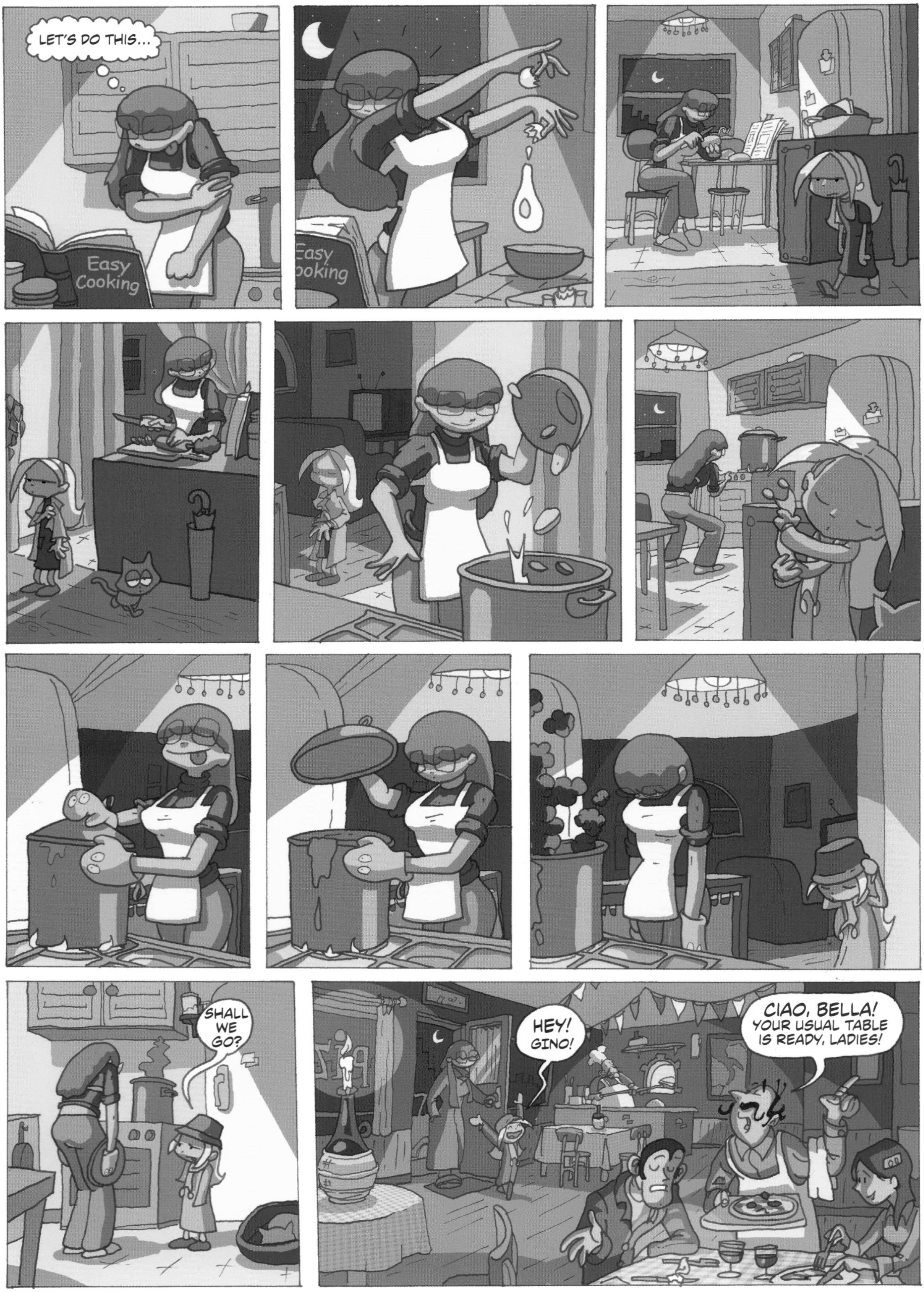
LET'S DO THIS...
Easy Cooking
Easy ooking
SHALL WE GO?
HEY! GINO!
CIAO, BELLA! YOUR USUAL TABLE IS READY, LADIES!

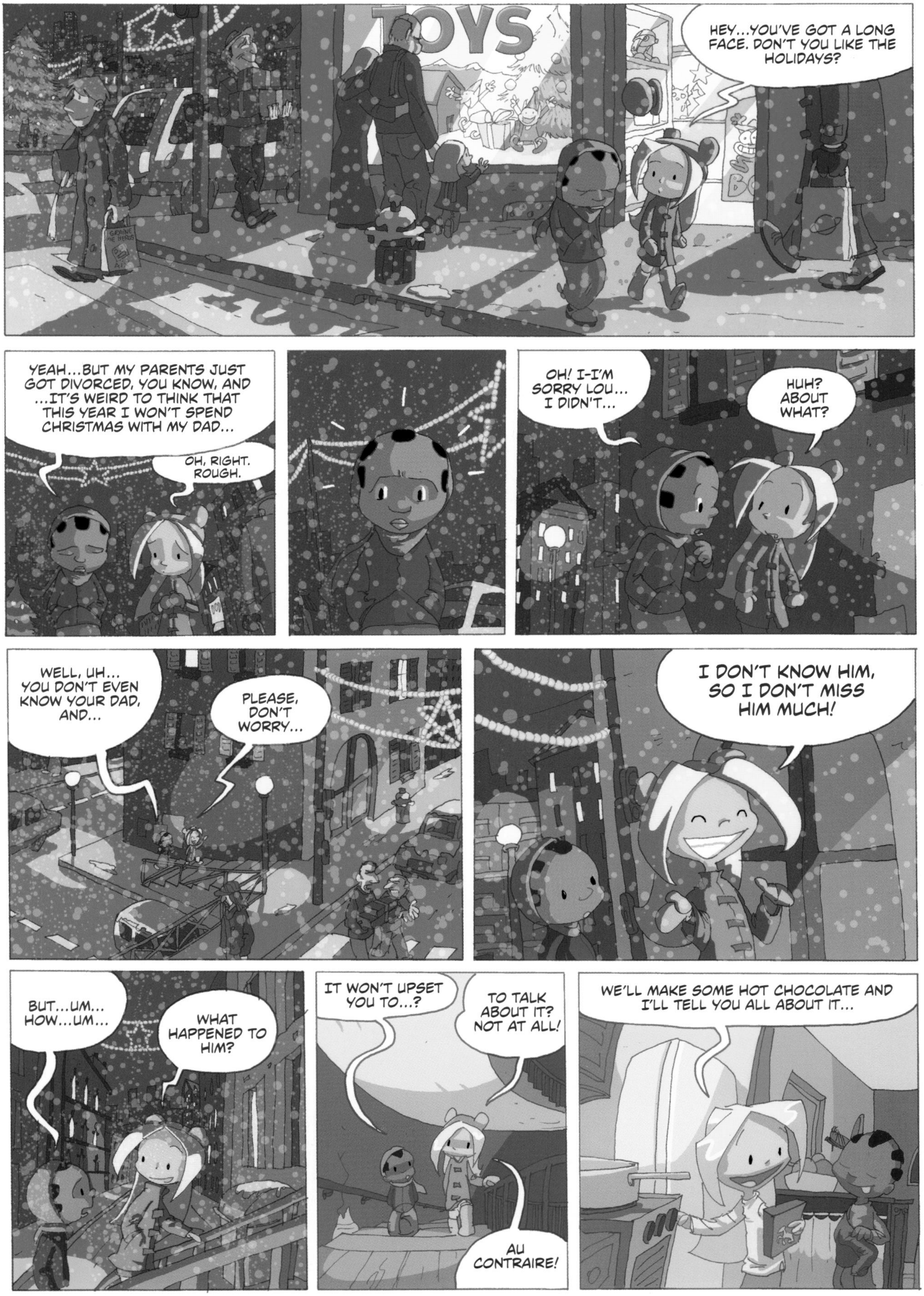
TOYS
HEY...YOU'VE GOT A LONG FACE. DON'T YOU LIKE THE HOLIDAYS?
YEAH...BUT MY PARENTS JUST GOT DIVORCED, YOU KNOW, AND ...IT'S WEIRD TO THINK THAT THIS YEAR I WON'T SPEND CHRISTMAS WITH MY DAD...
OH, RIGHT. ROUGH.
OH! I-I'M SORRY LOU... I DIDN'T...
HUH? ABOUT WHAT?
WELL, UH... YOU DON'T EVEN KNOW YOUR DAD, AND...
PLEASE, DON'T WORRY...
I DON'T KNOW HIM, SO I DON'T MISS HIM MUCH!
BUT...UM... HOW...UM...
WHAT HAPPENED TO HIM?
IT WON'T UPSET YOU TO...?
TO TALK ABOUT IT? NOT AT ALL!
AU CONTRAIRE!
WE'LL MAKE SOME HOT CHOCOLATE AND I'LL TELL YOU ALL ABOUT IT...

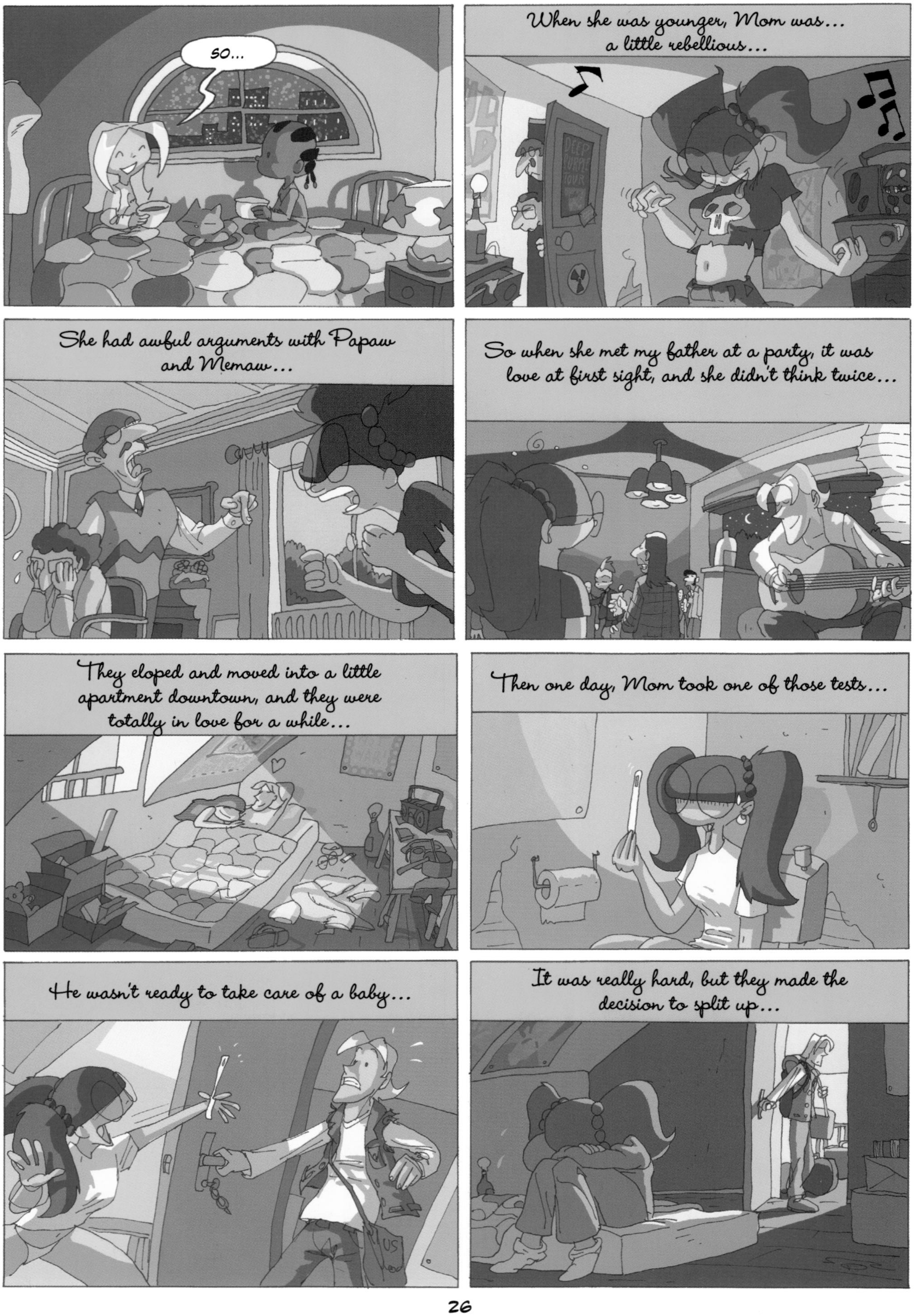

SO...
When she was younger, Mom was... a little rebellious...
She had awful arguments with Papaw and Memaw...
So when she met my father at a party, it was love at first sight, and she didn't think twice...
They eloped and moved into a little apartment downtown, and they were totally in love for a while...
Then one day, Mom took one of those tests...
He wasn't ready to take care of a baby...
It was really hard, but they made the decision to split up...

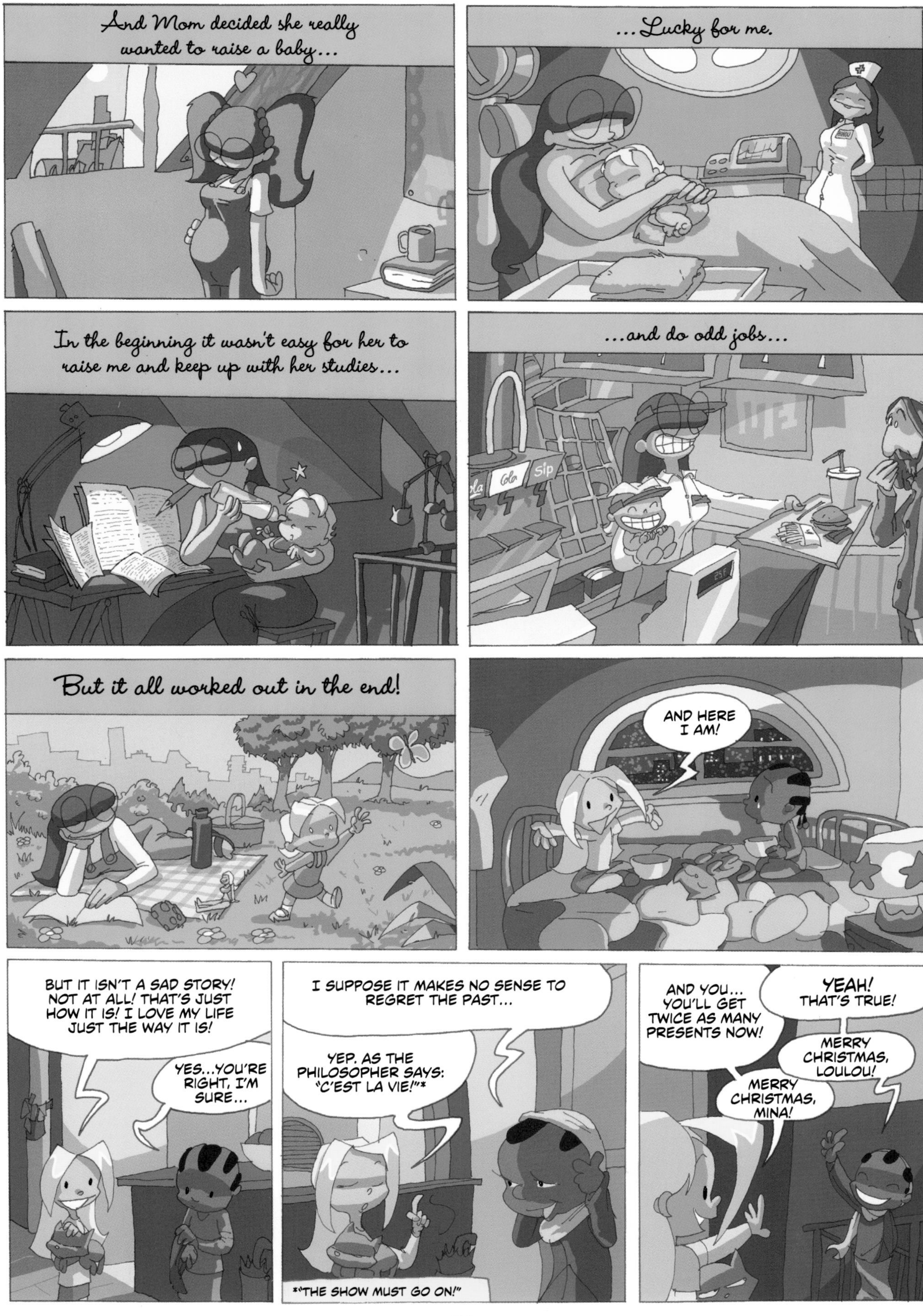
And Mom decided she really wanted to raise a baby...
...Lucky for me.
In the beginning it wasn't easy for her to raise me and keep up with her studies...
...and do odd jobs...
But it all worked out in the end!
AND HERE I AM!
BUT IT ISN'T A SAD STORY! NOT AT ALL! THAT'S JUST HOW IT IS! I LOVE MY LIFE JUST THE WAY IT IS!
YES...YOU'RE RIGHT, I'M SURE...
I SUPPOSE IT MAKES NO SENSE TO REGRET THE PAST...
YEP. AS THE PHILOSOPHER SAYS: "C'EST LA VIE!"*
*"THE SHOW MUST GO ON!"
AND YOU... YOU'LL GET TWICE AS MANY PRESENTS NOW!
YEAH! THAT'S TRUE!
MERRY CHRISTMAS, LOULOU!
MERRY CHRISTMAS, MINA!

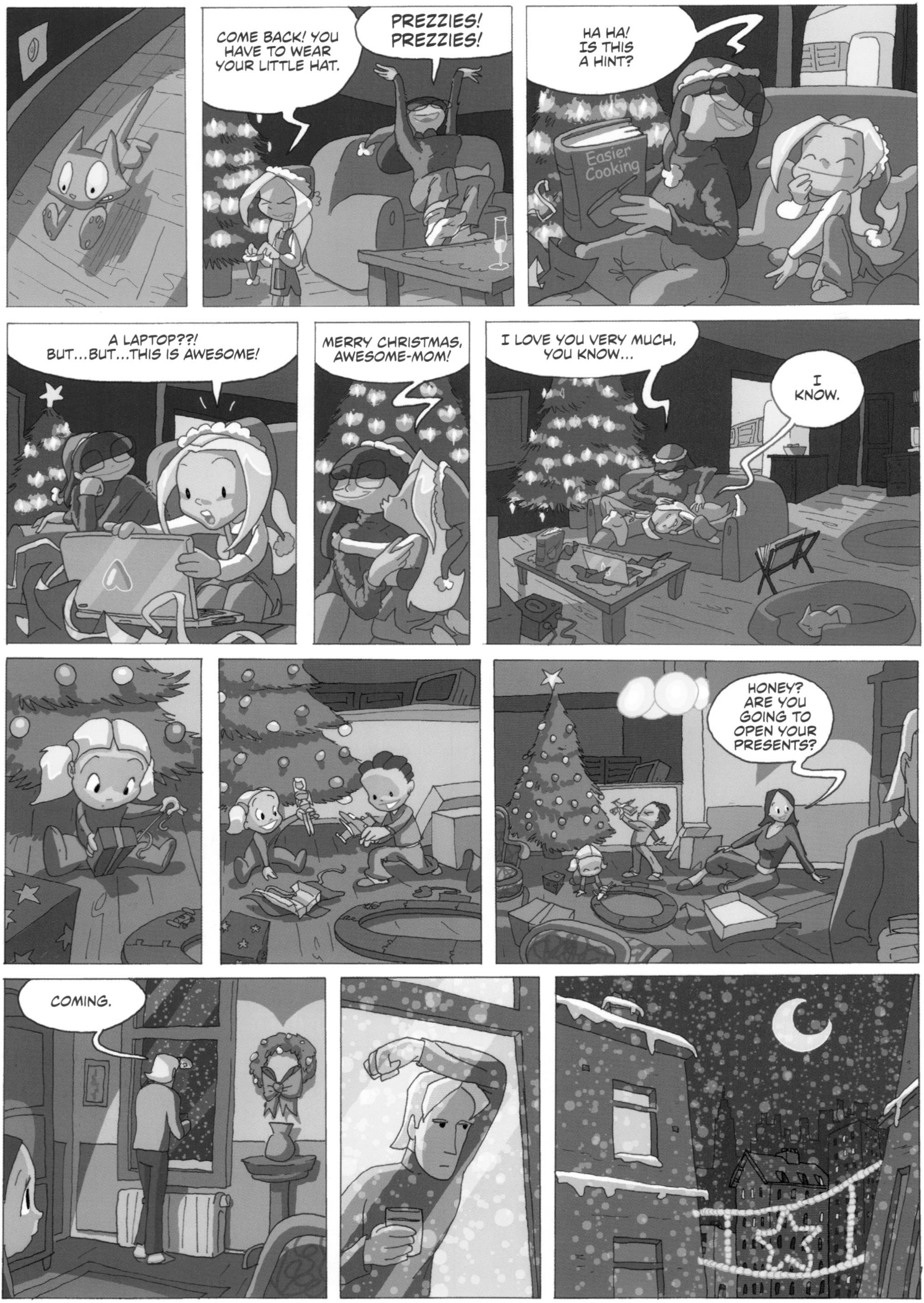

COME BACK! YOU HAVE TO WEAR YOUR LITTLE HAT.
PREZZIES! PREZZIES!
HA HA! IS THIS A HINT?
Easier Cooking
A LAPTOP??! BUT...BUT...THIS IS AWESOME!
MERRY CHRISTMAS, AWESOME-MOM!
I LOVE YOU VERY MUCH, YOU KNOW...
I KNOW.
HONEY? ARE YOU GOING TO OPEN YOUR PRESENTS?
COMING.

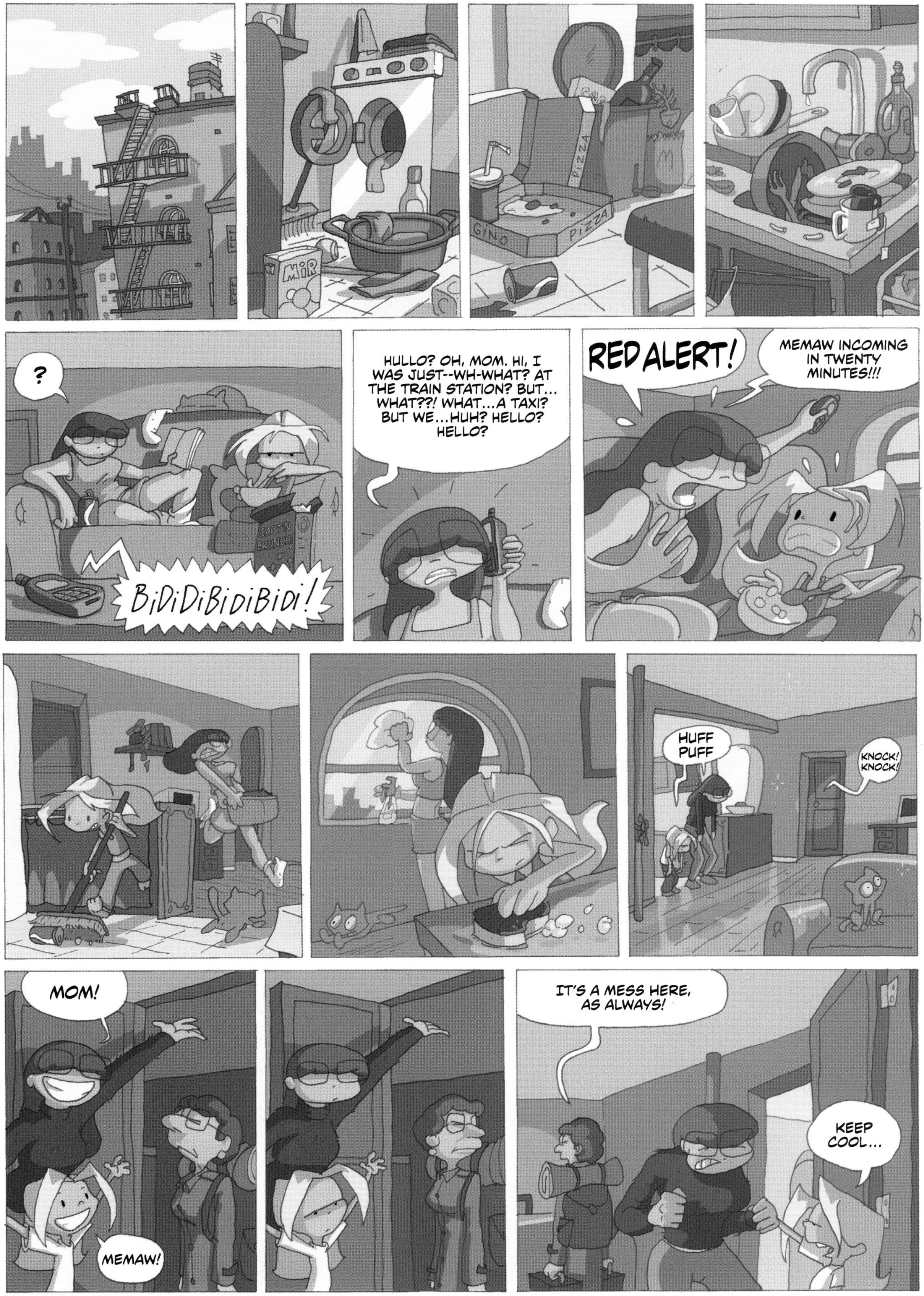
MIR
PIZZA
GINO
PIZZA
?
CAP'N BRUNCH!
BiDiDiBiDiBiDi!
HULLO? OH, MOM. HI, I WAS JUST--WH-WHAT? AT THE TRAIN STATION? BUT... WHAT??! WHAT...A TAXI? BUT WE...HUH? HELLO? HELLO?
RED ALERT!
MEMAW INCOMING IN TWENTY MINUTES!!!
HUFF PUFF
KNOCK! KNOCK!
MOM!
MEMAW!
IT'S A MESS HERE, AS ALWAYS!
KEEP COOL...

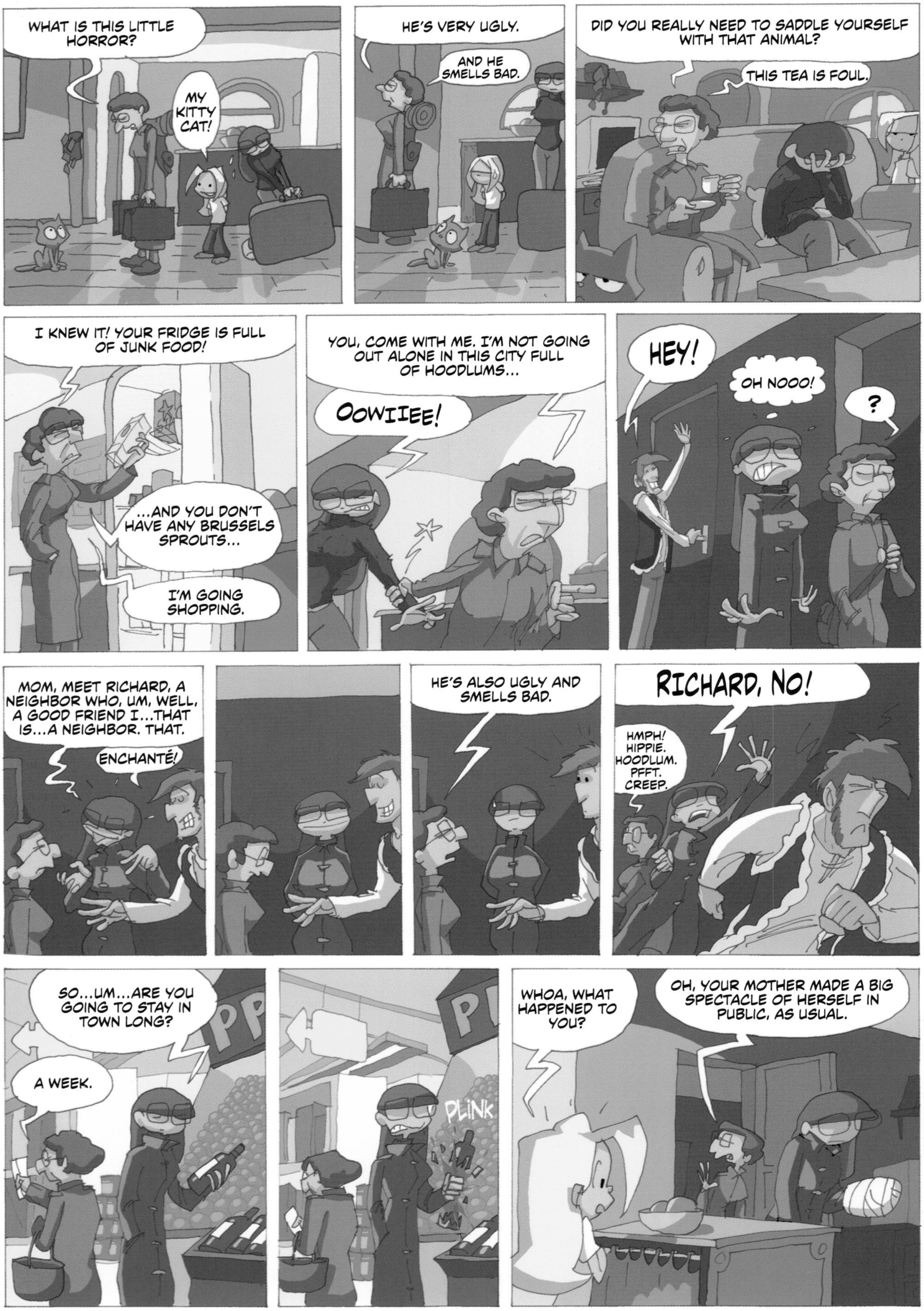

WHAT IS THIS LITTLE HORROR?
MY KITTY CAT!
HE'S VERY UGLY.
AND HE SMELLS BAD.
DID YOU REALLY NEED TO SADDLE YOURSELF WITH THAT ANIMAL?
THIS TEA IS FOUL.
I KNEW IT! YOUR FRIDGE IS FULL OF JUNK FOOD!
...AND YOU DON'T HAVE ANY BRUSSELS SPROUTS...
I'M GOING SHOPPING.
YOU, COME WITH ME. I'M NOT GOING OUT ALONE IN THIS CITY FULL OF HOODLUMS...
OOWIIEE!
HEY!
OH NOOO!
?
MOM, MEET RICHARD, A NEIGHBOR WHO, UM, WELL, A GOOD FRIEND I...THAT IS...A NEIGHBOR. THAT.
ENCHANTÉ!
HE'S ALSO UGLY AND SMELLS BAD.
RICHARD, NO!
HMPH! HIPPIE. HOODLUM. PFFT. CREEP.
SO...UM...ARE YOU GOING TO STAY IN TOWN LONG?
A WEEK.
PLINK
WHOA, WHAT HAPPENED TO YOU?
OH, YOUR MOTHER MADE A BIG SPECTACLE OF HERSELF IN PUBLIC, AS USUAL.

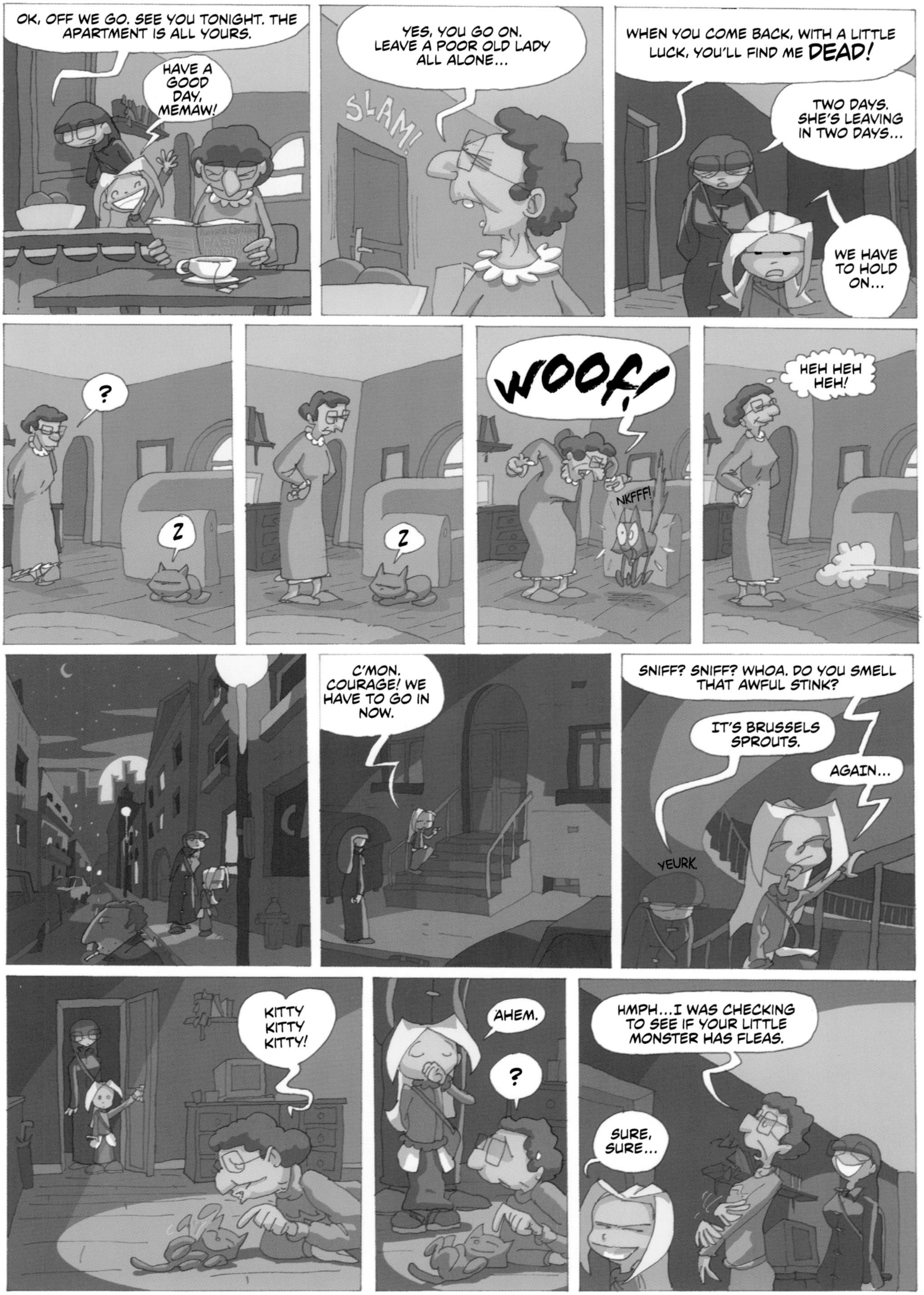
OK, OFF WE GO. SEE YOU TONIGHT. THE APARTMENT IS ALL YOURS.
HAVE A GOOD DAY, MEMAW!
SLAM!
YES, YOU GO ON. LEAVE A POOR OLD LADY ALL ALONE...
WHEN YOU COME BACK, WITH A LITTLE LUCK, YOU'LL FIND ME DEAD!
TWO DAYS. SHE'S LEAVING IN TWO DAYS...
WE HAVE TO HOLD ON...
?
Z
Z
WOOF!
NKFFF!
HEH HEH HEH!
C'MON. COURAGE! WE HAVE TO GO IN NOW.
SNIFF? SNIFF? WHOA. DO YOU SMELL THAT AWFUL STINK?
IT'S BRUSSELS SPROUTS.
AGAIN...
YEURK.
KITTY KITTY KITTY!
AHEM.
?
HMPH...I WAS CHECKING TO SEE IF YOUR LITTLE MONSTER HAS FLEAS.
SURE, SURE...

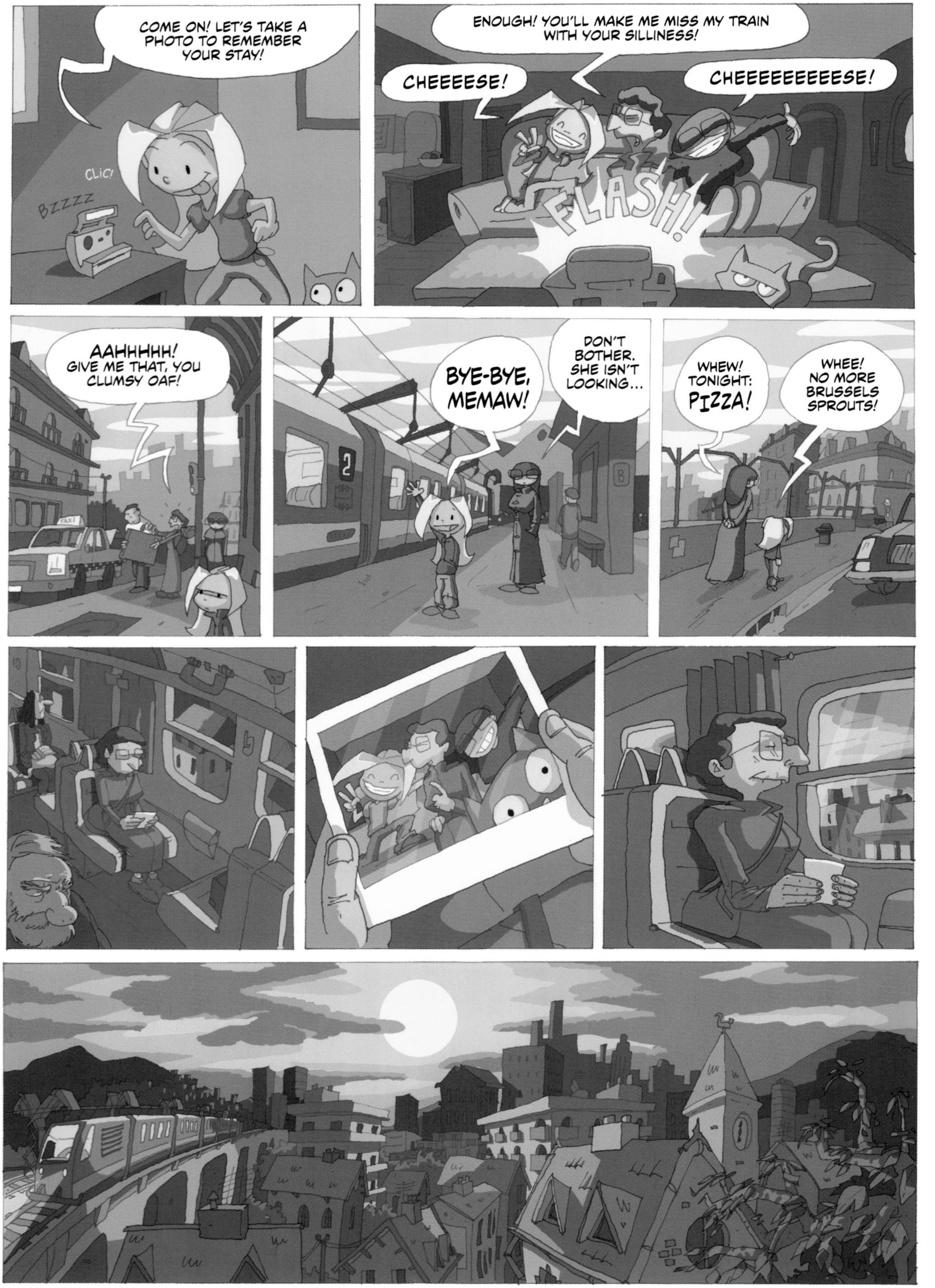
COME ON! LET'S TAKE A PHOTO TO REMEMBER YOUR STAY!
CLIC!
BZZZZ
ENOUGH! YOU'LL MAKE ME MISS MY TRAIN WITH YOUR SILLINESS!
CHEEEESE!
CHEEEEEEEEESE!
FLASH!
AAHHHHH! GIVE ME THAT, YOU CLUMSY OAF!
TAXI
BYE-BYE, MEMAW!
DON'T BOTHER. SHE ISN'T LOOKING...
WHEW! TONIGHT: PIZZA!
WHEE! NO MORE BRUSSELS SPROUTS!

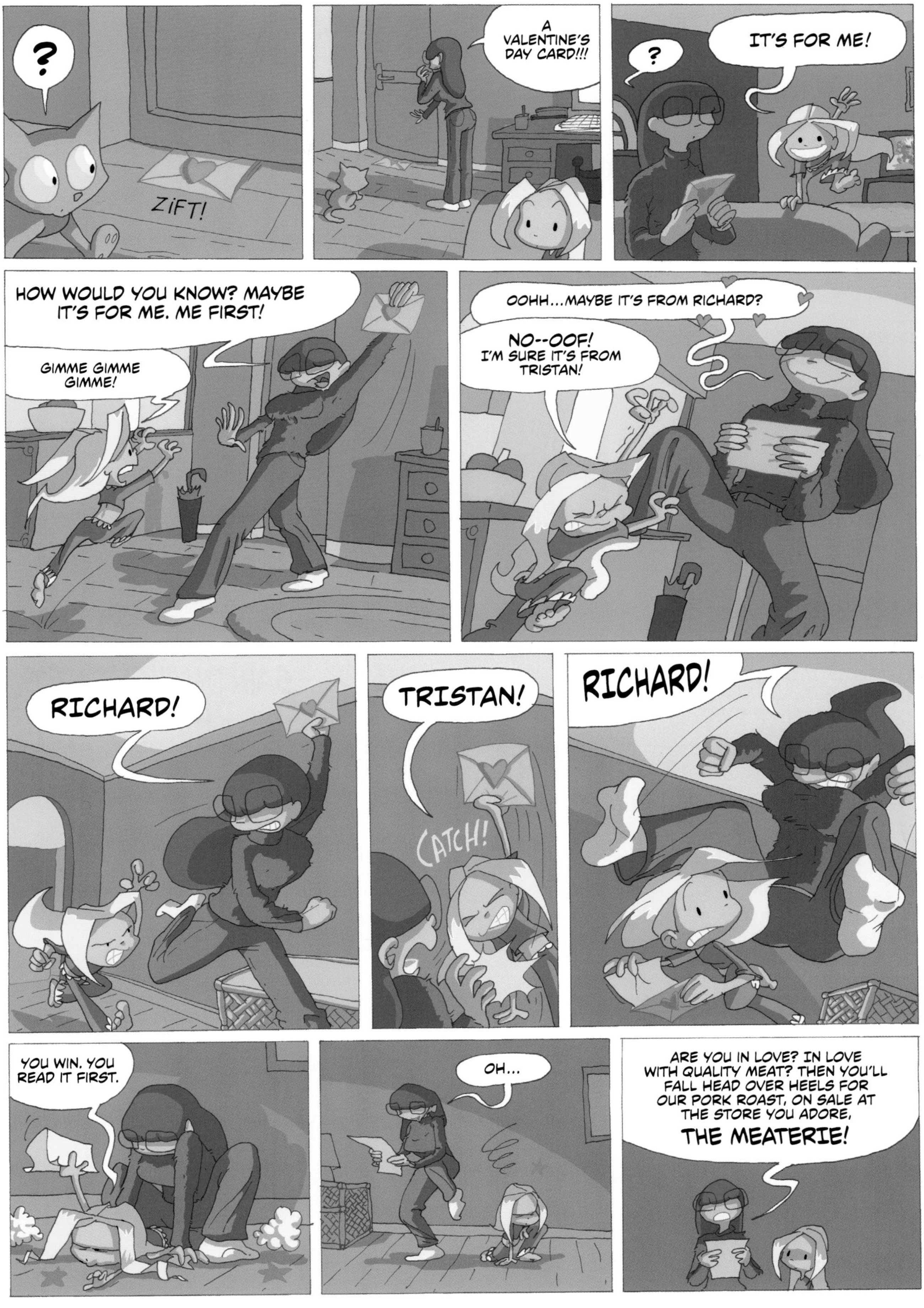
?
ZIFT!
A VALENTINE'S DAY CARD!!!
?
IT'S FOR ME!
HOW WOULD YOU KNOW? MAYBE IT'S FOR ME. ME FIRST!
GIMME GIMME GIMME!
OOHH...MAYBE IT'S FROM RICHARD?
NO--OOF! I'M SURE IT'S FROM TRISTAN!
RICHARD!
TRISTAN!
CATCH!
RICHARD!
YOU WIN. YOU READ IT FIRST.
OH...
ARE YOU IN LOVE? IN LOVE WITH QUALITY MEAT? THEN YOU'LL FALL HEAD OVER HEELS FOR OUR PORK ROAST, ON SALE AT THE STORE YOU ADORE,
THE MEATERIE!

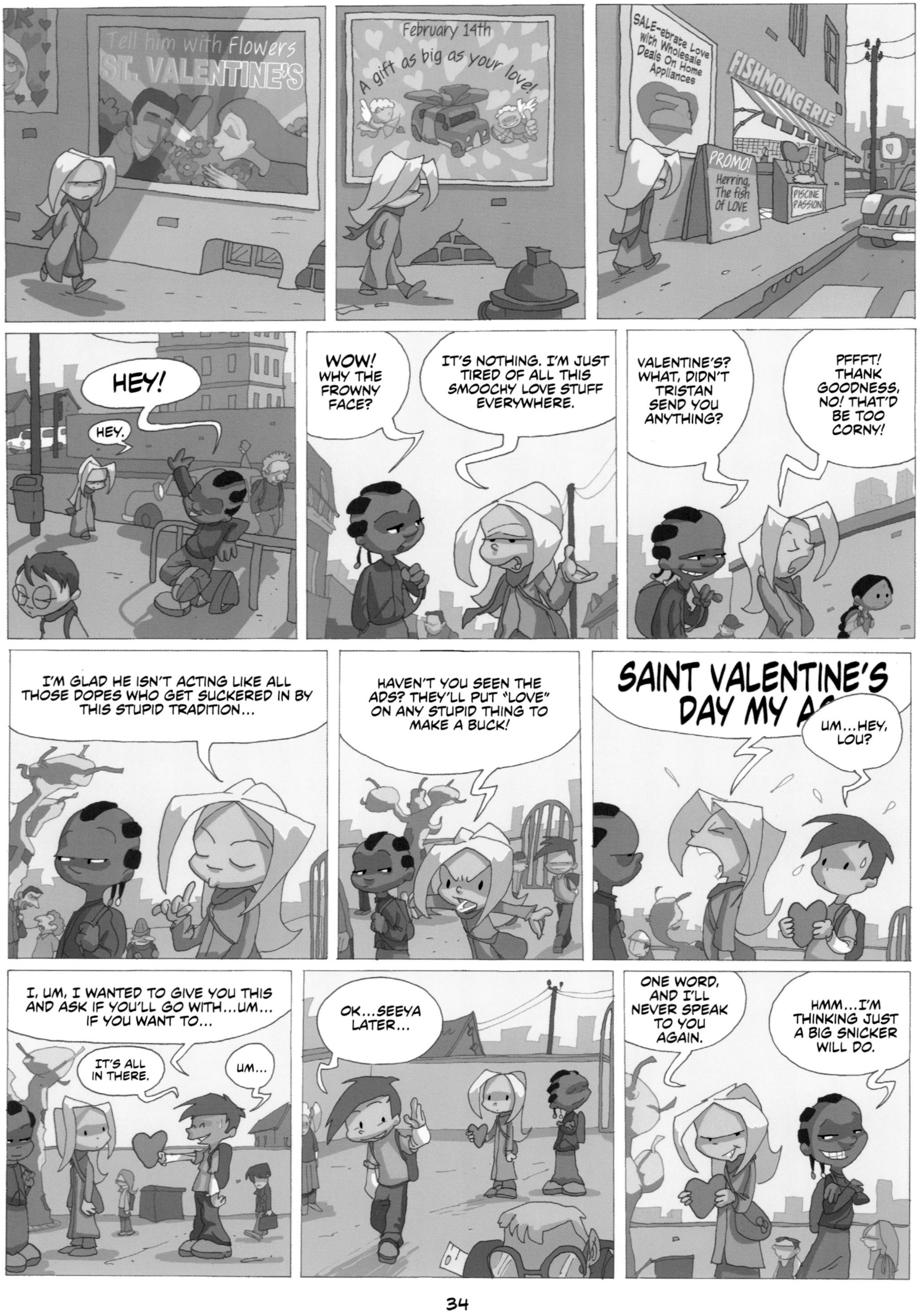
Tell him with Flowers
ST. VALENTINE'S
February 14th
A gift as big as your love!
SALE-ebrate Love With Wholesale Deals On Home Appliances
FISHMONGERIE
PROMO! Herring, The fish Of LOVE
PISCINE PASSION
HEY!
HEY.
WOW! WHY THE FROWNY FACE?
IT'S NOTHING. I'M JUST TIRED OF ALL THIS SMOOCHY LOVE STUFF EVERYWHERE.
VALENTINE'S? WHAT, DIDN'T TRISTAN SEND YOU ANYTHING?
PFFFT! THANK GOODNESS, NO! THAT'D BE TOO CORNY!
I'M GLAD HE ISN'T ACTING LIKE ALL THOSE DOPES WHO GET SUCKERED IN BY THIS STUPID TRADITION...
HAVEN'T YOU SEEN THE ADS? THEY'LL PUT "LOVE" ON ANY STUPID THING TO MAKE A BUCK!
SAINT VALENTINE'S DAY MY A
UM...HEY, LOU?
I, UM, I WANTED TO GIVE YOU THIS AND ASK IF YOU'LL GO WITH...UM... IF YOU WANT TO...
IT'S ALL IN THERE.
UM...
OK...SEEYA LATER...
ONE WORD, AND I'LL NEVER SPEAK TO YOU AGAIN.
HMM...I'M THINKING JUST A BIG SNICKER WILL DO.

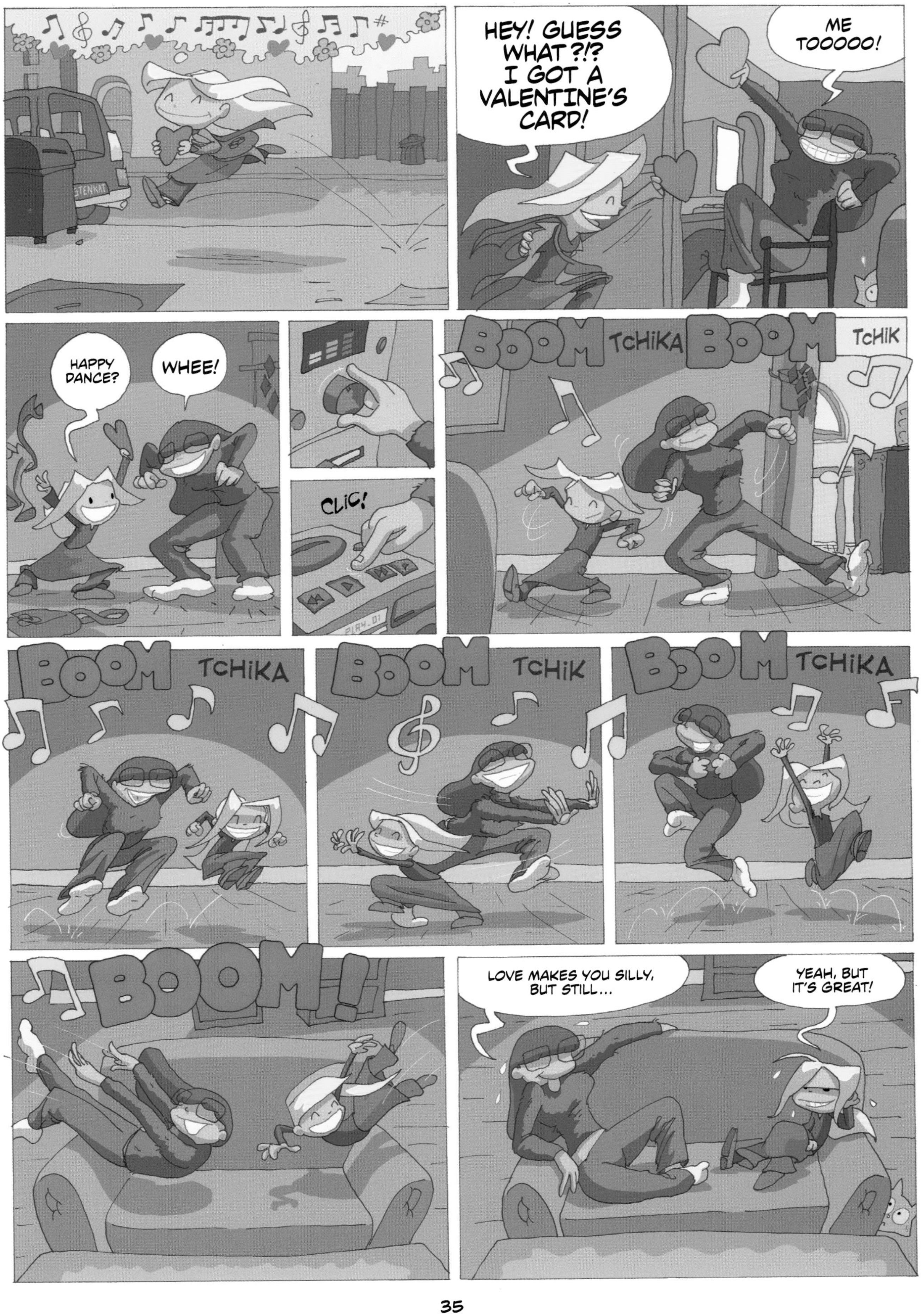
STENKAT
HEY! GUESS WHAT ?!? I GOT A VALENTINE'S CARD!
ME TOOOOO!
HAPPY DANCE?
WHEE!
CLIC!
BOOM TCHIKA BOOM TCHIK
BOOM TCHIKA
BOOM TCHIK
BOOM TCHIKA
BOOM!
LOVE MAKES YOU SILLY, BUT STILL...
YEAH, BUT IT'S GREAT!

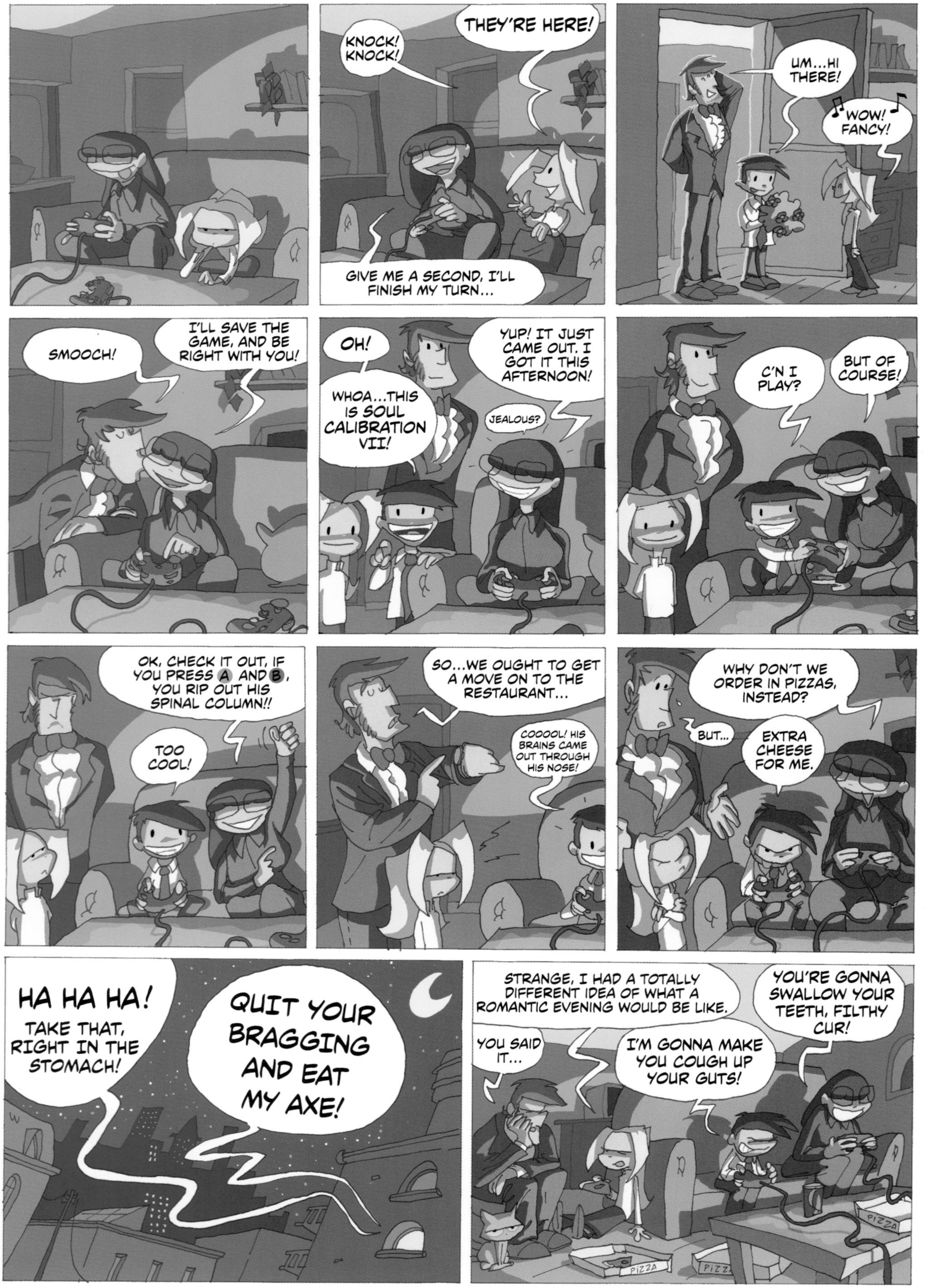
KNOCK! KNOCK!
THEY'RE HERE!
GIVE ME A SECOND, I'LL FINISH MY TURN...
UM...HI THERE!
WOW! FANCY!
SMOOCH!
I'LL SAVE THE GAME, AND BE RIGHT WITH YOU!
OH!
WHOA...THIS IS SOUL CALIBRATION VII!
YUP! IT JUST CAME OUT. I GOT IT THIS AFTERNOON!
JEALOUS?
C'N I PLAY?
BUT OF COURSE!
OK, CHECK IT OUT, IF YOU PRESS A AND B, YOU RIP OUT HIS SPINAL COLUMN!!
TOO COOL!
SO...WE OUGHT TO GET A MOVE ON TO THE RESTAURANT...
COOOOL! HIS BRAINS CAME OUT THROUGH HIS NOSE!
WHY DON'T WE ORDER IN PIZZAS, INSTEAD?
BUT...
EXTRA CHEESE FOR ME.
HA HA HA! TAKE THAT, RIGHT IN THE STOMACH!
QUIT YOUR BRAGGING AND EAT MY AXE!
STRANGE, I HAD A TOTALLY DIFFERENT IDEA OF WHAT A ROMANTIC EVENING WOULD BE LIKE.
YOU SAID IT...
I'M GONNA MAKE YOU COUGH UP YOUR GUTS!
YOU'RE GONNA SWALLOW YOUR TEETH, FILTHY CUR!
PIZZA
PIZZA
PIZZA

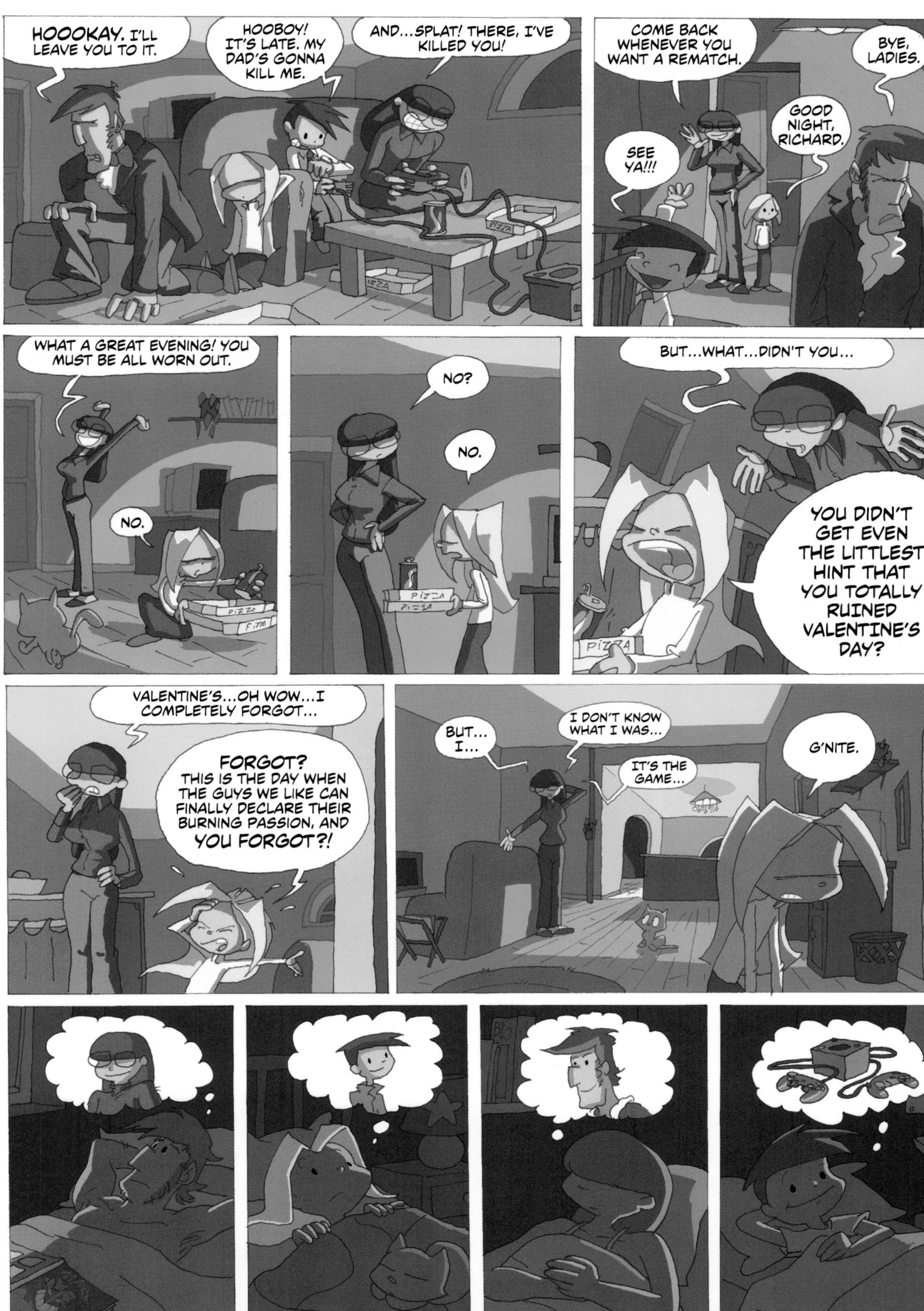

HOOOKAY. I'LL LEAVE YOU TO IT.
HOOBOY! IT'S LATE. MY DAD'S GONNA KILL ME.
AND...SPLAT! THERE, I'VE KILLED YOU!
PIZZA
COME BACK WHENEVER YOU WANT A REMATCH.
BYE, LADIES.
GOOD NIGHT, RICHARD.
SEE YA!!!
WHAT A GREAT EVENING! YOU MUST BE ALL WORN OUT.
NO.
NO?
NO.
BUT...WHAT...DIDN'T YOU...
YOU DIDN'T GET EVEN THE LITTLEST HINT THAT YOU TOTALLY RUINED VALENTINE'S DAY?
VALENTINE'S...OH WOW...I COMPLETELY FORGOT...
FORGOT? THIS IS THE DAY WHEN THE GUYS WE LIKE CAN FINALLY DECLARE THEIR BURNING PASSION, AND YOU FORGOT?!
BUT... I...
I DON'T KNOW WHAT I WAS...
IT'S THE GAME...
G'NITE.

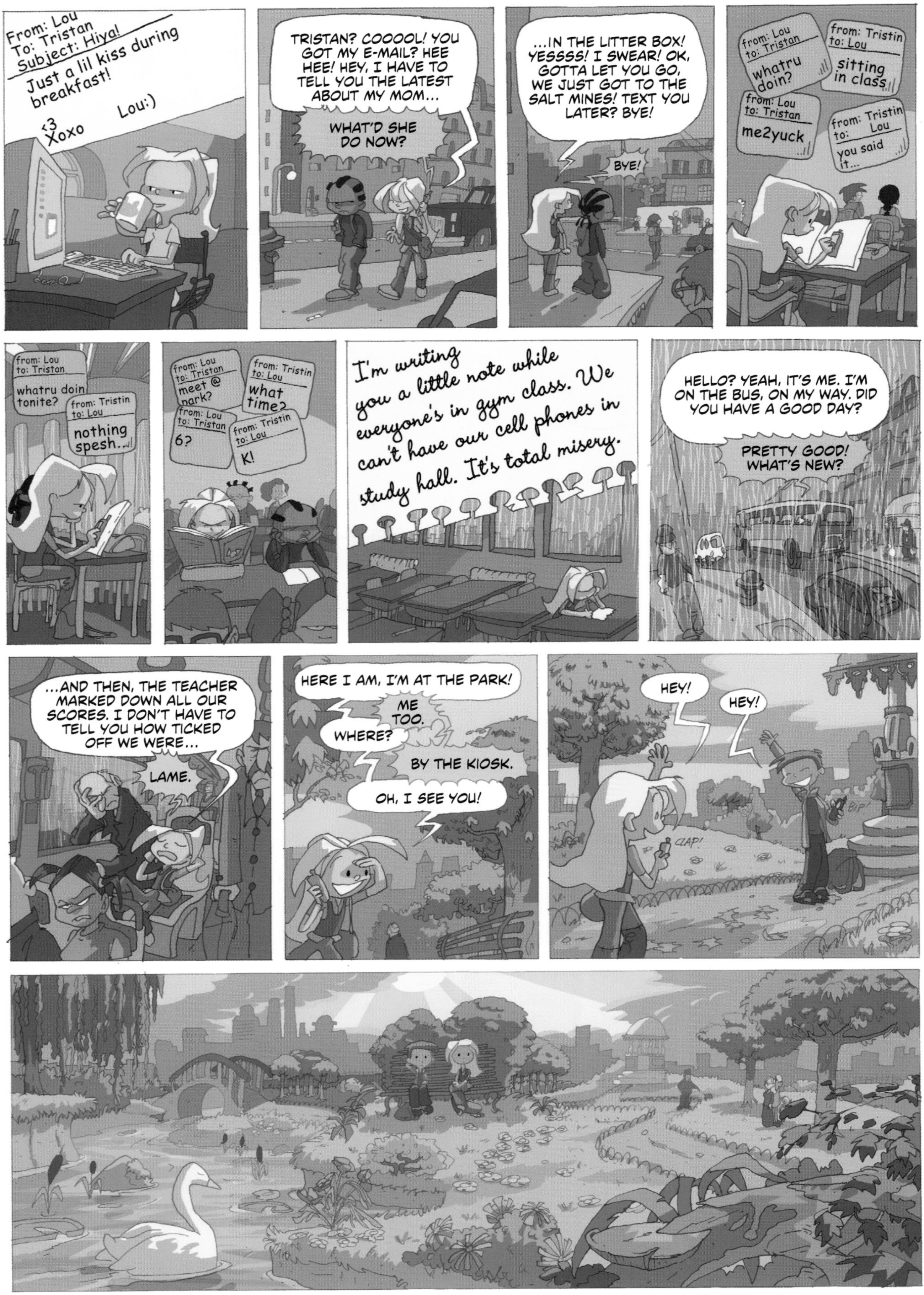
From: Lou
To: Tristan
Subject: Hiya!
Just a lil kiss during breakfast!
<3 Xoxo Lou:)
TRISTAN? COOOOL! YOU GOT MY E-MAIL? HEE HEE! HEY, I HAVE TO TELL YOU THE LATEST ABOUT MY MOM...
WHAT'D SHE DO NOW?
...IN THE LITTER BOX! YESSSS! I SWEAR! OK, GOTTA LET YOU GO, WE JUST GOT TO THE SALT MINES! TEXT YOU LATER? BYE!
BYE!
from: Lou to: Tristan whatru doin?
from: Tristin to: Lou sitting in class
from: Lou to: Tristan me2yuck
from: Tristin to: Lou you said it...
from: Lou to: Tristan whatru doin tonite?
from: Tristin to: Lou nothing spesh...
from: Lou to: Tristan meet @ park?
from: Tristin to: Lou what time?
from: Lou to: Tristan 6?
from: Tristin to: Lou K!
I'm writing you a little note while everyone's in gym class. We can't have our cell phones in study hall. It's total misery.
HELLO? YEAH, IT'S ME. I'M ON THE BUS, ON MY WAY. DID YOU HAVE A GOOD DAY?
PRETTY GOOD! WHAT'S NEW?
...AND THEN, THE TEACHER MARKED DOWN ALL OUR SCORES. I DON'T HAVE TO TELL YOU HOW TICKED OFF WE WERE...
LAME.
HERE I AM, I'M AT THE PARK!
ME TOO.
WHERE?
BY THE KIOSK.
OH, I SEE YOU!
HEY!
HEY!
CLAP!
BIP!

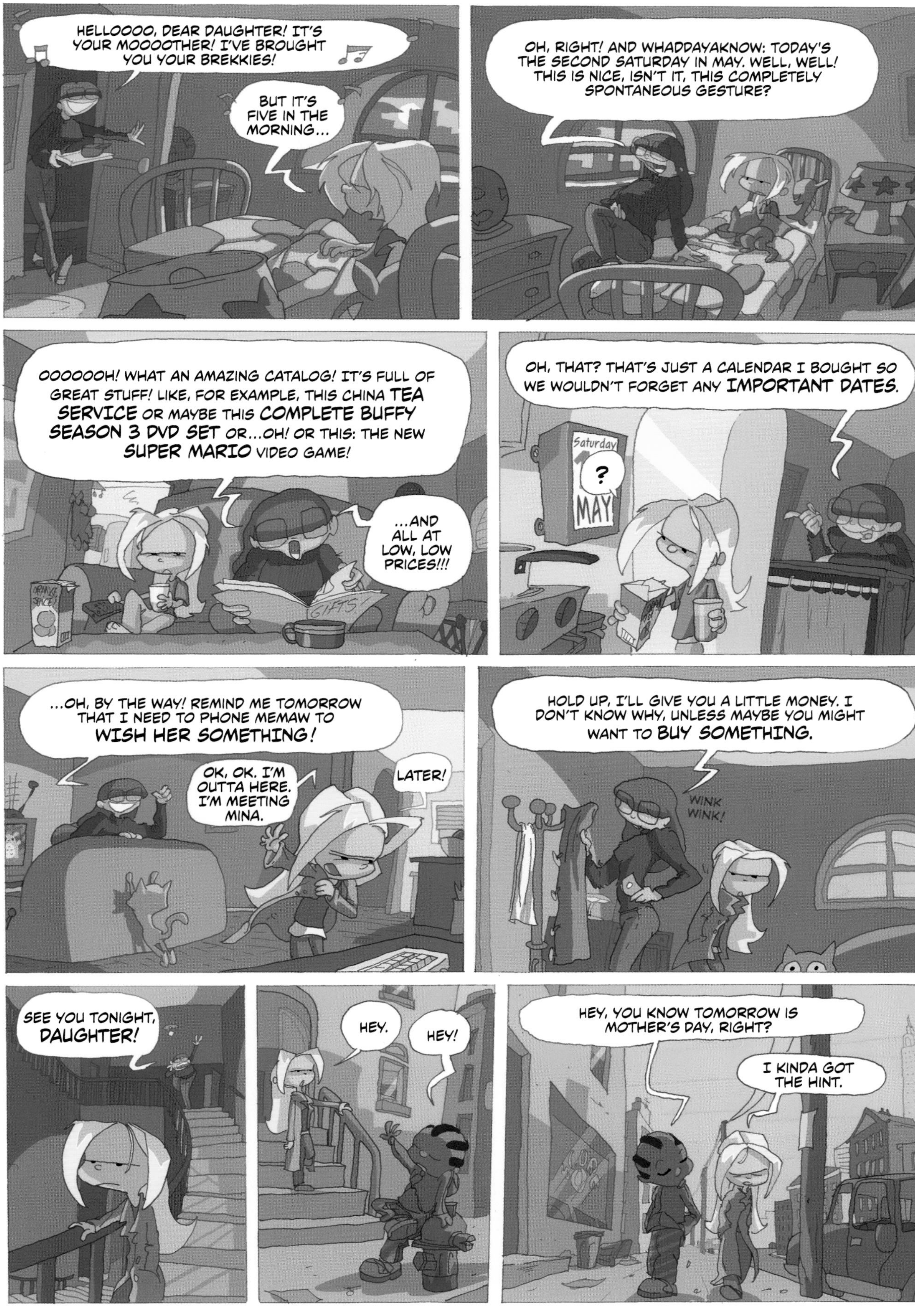

HELLOOOO, DEAR DAUGHTER! IT'S YOUR MOOOOTHER! I'VE BROUGHT YOU YOUR BREKKIES!
BUT IT'S FIVE IN THE MORNING...
OH, RIGHT! AND WHADDAYAKNOW: TODAY'S THE SECOND SATURDAY IN MAY. WELL, WELL! THIS IS NICE, ISN'T IT, THIS COMPLETELY SPONTANEOUS GESTURE?
OOOOOOH! WHAT AN AMAZING CATALOG! IT'S FULL OF GREAT STUFF! LIKE, FOR EXAMPLE, THIS CHINA TEA SERVICE OR MAYBE THIS COMPLETE BUFFY SEASON 3 DVD SET OR...OH! OR THIS: THE NEW SUPER MARIO VIDEO GAME!
...AND ALL AT LOW, LOW PRICES!!!
GIFTS!
ORANGE JUICE!
OH, THAT? THAT'S JUST A CALENDAR I BOUGHT SO WE WOULDN'T FORGET ANY IMPORTANT DATES.
Saturday
?
MAY
...OH, BY THE WAY! REMIND ME TOMORROW THAT I NEED TO PHONE MEMAW TO WISH HER SOMETHING!
OK, OK. I'M OUTTA HERE. I'M MEETING MINA.
LATER!
HOLD UP, I'LL GIVE YOU A LITTLE MONEY. I DON'T KNOW WHY, UNLESS MAYBE YOU MIGHT WANT TO BUY SOMETHING.
WINK WINK!
SEE YOU TONIGHT, DAUGHTER!
HEY.
HEY!
HEY, YOU KNOW TOMORROW IS MOTHER'S DAY, RIGHT?
I KINDA GOT THE HINT.

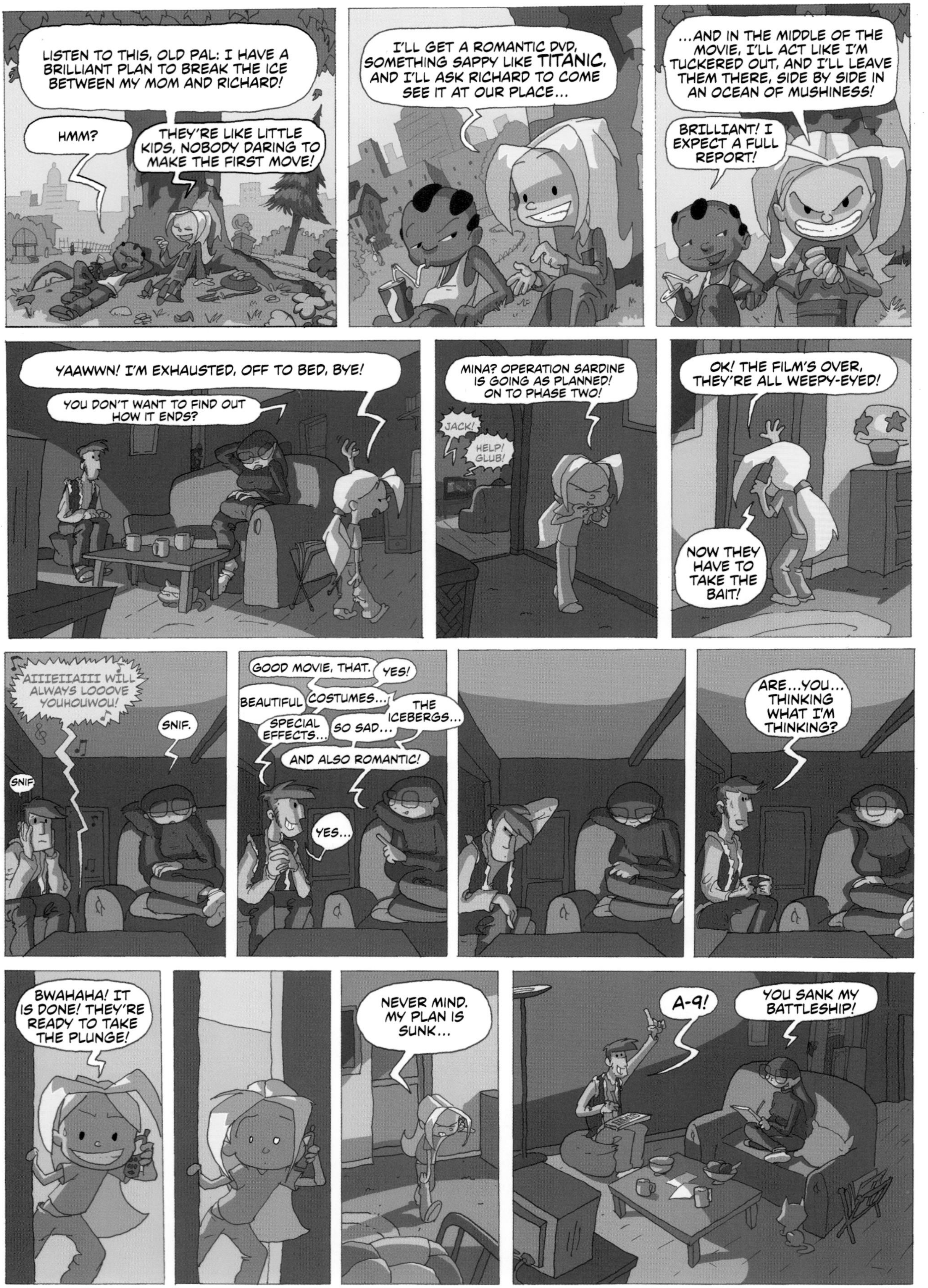
LISTEN TO THIS, OLD PAL: I HAVE A BRILLIANT PLAN TO BREAK THE ICE BETWEEN MY MOM AND RICHARD!
HMM?
THEY'RE LIKE LITTLE KIDS, NOBODY DARING TO MAKE THE FIRST MOVE!
I'LL GET A ROMANTIC DVD, SOMETHING SAPPY LIKE TITANIC, AND I'LL ASK RICHARD TO COME SEE IT AT OUR PLACE...
...AND IN THE MIDDLE OF THE MOVIE, I'LL ACT LIKE I'M TUCKERED OUT, AND I'LL LEAVE THEM THERE, SIDE BY SIDE IN AN OCEAN OF MUSHINESS!
BRILLIANT! I EXPECT A FULL REPORT!
YAAWWN! I'M EXHAUSTED, OFF TO BED, BYE!
YOU DON'T WANT TO FIND OUT HOW IT ENDS?
MINA? OPERATION SARDINE IS GOING AS PLANNED! ON TO PHASE TWO!
JACK!
HELP! GLUB!
OK! THE FILM'S OVER, THEY'RE ALL WEEPY-EYED!
NOW THEY HAVE TO TAKE THE BAIT!
AIIIEIIAIII WILL ALWAYS LOOOVE YOUHOUWOU!
SNIF.
SNIF
GOOD MOVIE, THAT.
YES!
BEAUTIFUL
COSTUMES...
THE ICEBERGS...
SPECIAL EFFECTS...
SO SAD...
AND ALSO ROMANTIC!
YES...
ARE...YOU... THINKING WHAT I'M THINKING?
BWAHAHA! IT IS DONE! THEY'RE READY TO TAKE THE PLUNGE!
NEVER MIND. MY PLAN IS SUNK...
A-9!
YOU SANK MY BATTLESHIP!

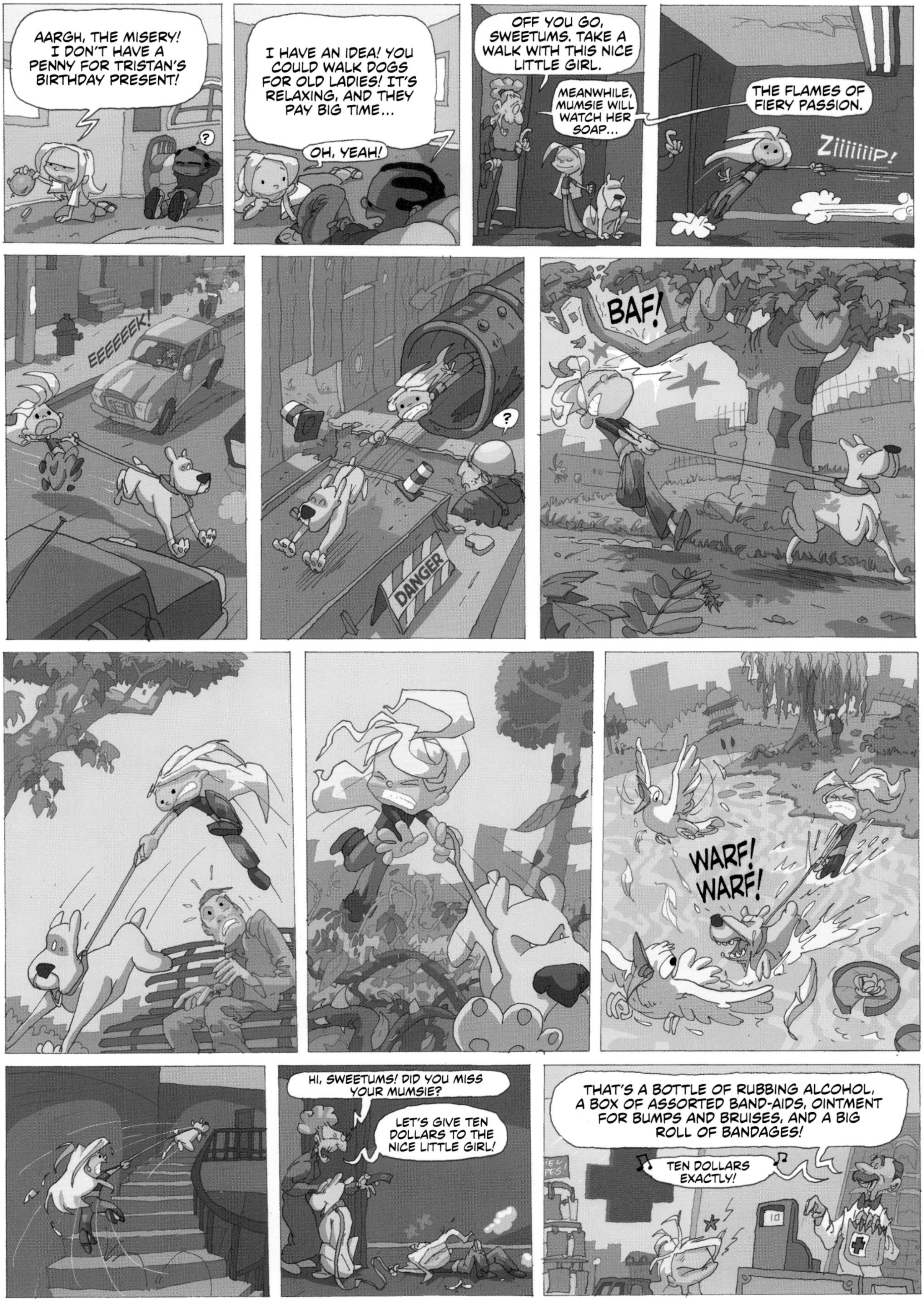
AARGH, THE MISERY! I DON'T HAVE A PENNY FOR TRISTAN'S BIRTHDAY PRESENT!
?
I HAVE AN IDEA! YOU COULD WALK DOGS FOR OLD LADIES! IT'S RELAXING, AND THEY PAY BIG TIME...
OH, YEAH!
OFF YOU GO, SWEETUMS. TAKE A WALK WITH THIS NICE LITTLE GIRL.
MEANWHILE, MUMSIE WILL WATCH HER SOAP...
THE FLAMES OF FIERY PASSION.
ZIIIIIIP!
EEEEEEK!
?
DANGER
BAF!
WARF! WARF!
HI, SWEETUMS! DID YOU MISS YOUR MUMSIE?
LET'S GIVE TEN DOLLARS TO THE NICE LITTLE GIRL!
THAT'S A BOTTLE OF RUBBING ALCOHOL, A BOX OF ASSORTED BAND-AIDS, OINTMENT FOR BUMPS AND BRUISES, AND A BIG ROLL OF BANDAGES!
TEN DOLLARS EXACTLY!

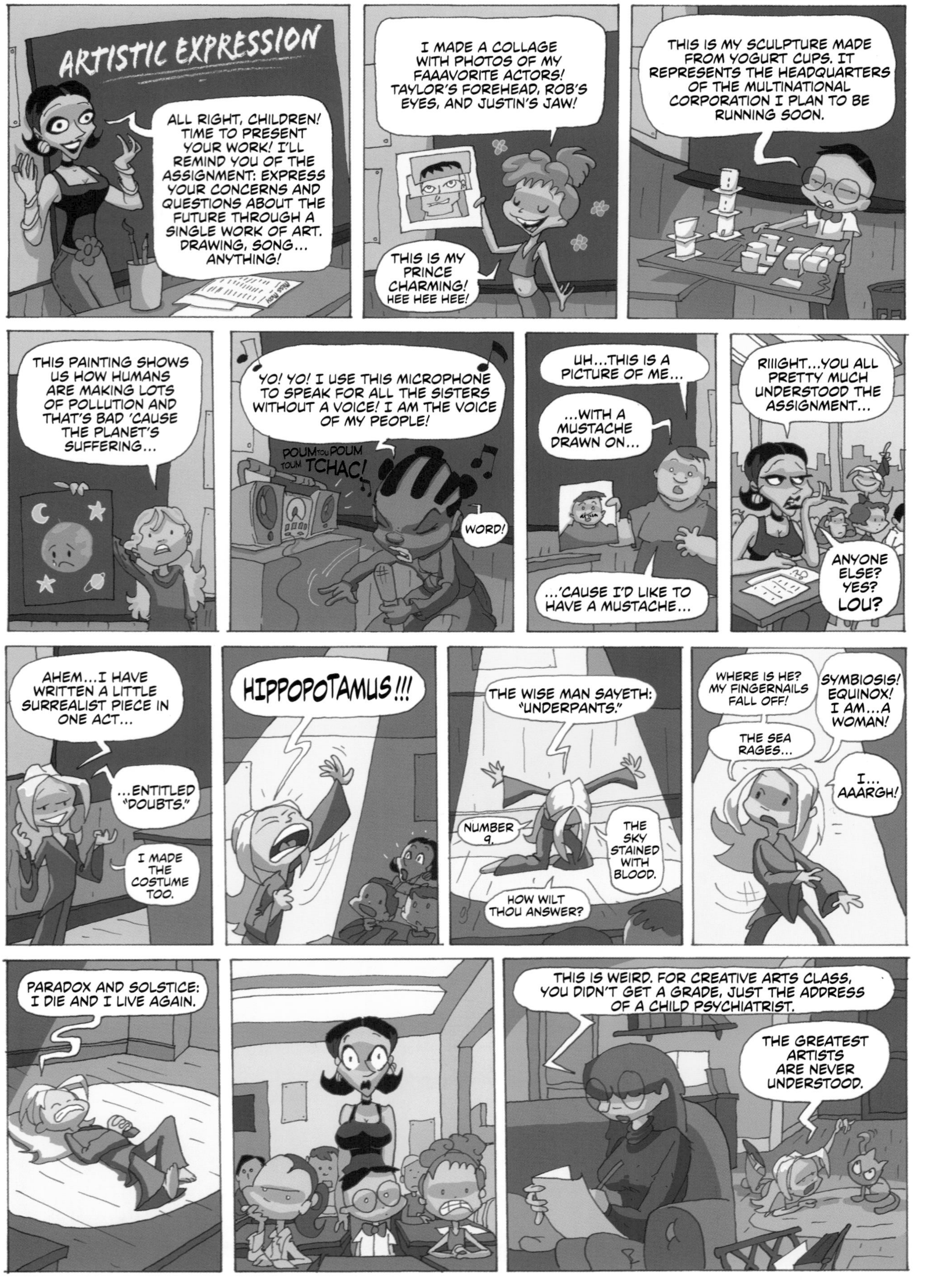
ARTISTIC EXPRESSION
ALL RIGHT, CHILDREN! TIME TO PRESENT YOUR WORK! I'LL REMIND YOU OF THE ASSIGNMENT: EXPRESS YOUR CONCERNS AND QUESTIONS ABOUT THE FUTURE THROUGH A SINGLE WORK OF ART. DRAWING, SONG... ANYTHING!
I MADE A COLLAGE WITH PHOTOS OF MY FAAAVORITE ACTORS! TAYLOR'S FOREHEAD, ROB'S EYES, AND JUSTIN'S JAW!
THIS IS MY PRINCE CHARMING! HEE HEE HEE!
THIS IS MY SCULPTURE MADE FROM YOGURT CUPS. IT REPRESENTS THE HEADQUARTERS OF THE MULTINATIONAL CORPORATION I PLAN TO BE RUNNING SOON.
THIS PAINTING SHOWS US HOW HUMANS ARE MAKING LOTS OF POLLUTION AND THAT'S BAD 'CAUSE THE PLANET'S SUFFERING...
YO! YO! I USE THIS MICROPHONE TO SPEAK FOR ALL THE SISTERS WITHOUT A VOICE! I AM THE VOICE OF MY PEOPLE!
POUM TOU POUM TOUM TCHAC!
WORD!
UH...THIS IS A PICTURE OF ME...
...WITH A MUSTACHE DRAWN ON...
...'CAUSE I'D LIKE TO HAVE A MUSTACHE...
RIIIGHT...YOU ALL PRETTY MUCH UNDERSTOOD THE ASSIGNMENT...
ANYONE ELSE? YES? LOU?
AHEM...I HAVE WRITTEN A LITTLE SURREALIST PIECE IN ONE ACT...
...ENTITLED "DOUBTS."
I MADE THE COSTUME TOO.
HIPPOPOTAMUS!!!
THE WISE MAN SAYETH: "UNDERPANTS."
NUMBER 9.
THE SKY STAINED WITH BLOOD.
HOW WILT THOU ANSWER?
WHERE IS HE? MY FINGERNAILS FALL OFF!
SYMBIOSIS! EQUINOX! I AM...A WOMAN!
THE SEA RAGES...
I... AAARGH!
PARADOX AND SOLSTICE: I DIE AND I LIVE AGAIN.
THIS IS WEIRD. FOR CREATIVE ARTS CLASS, YOU DIDN'T GET A GRADE, JUST THE ADDRESS OF A CHILD PSYCHIATRIST.
THE GREATEST ARTISTS ARE NEVER UNDERSTOOD.

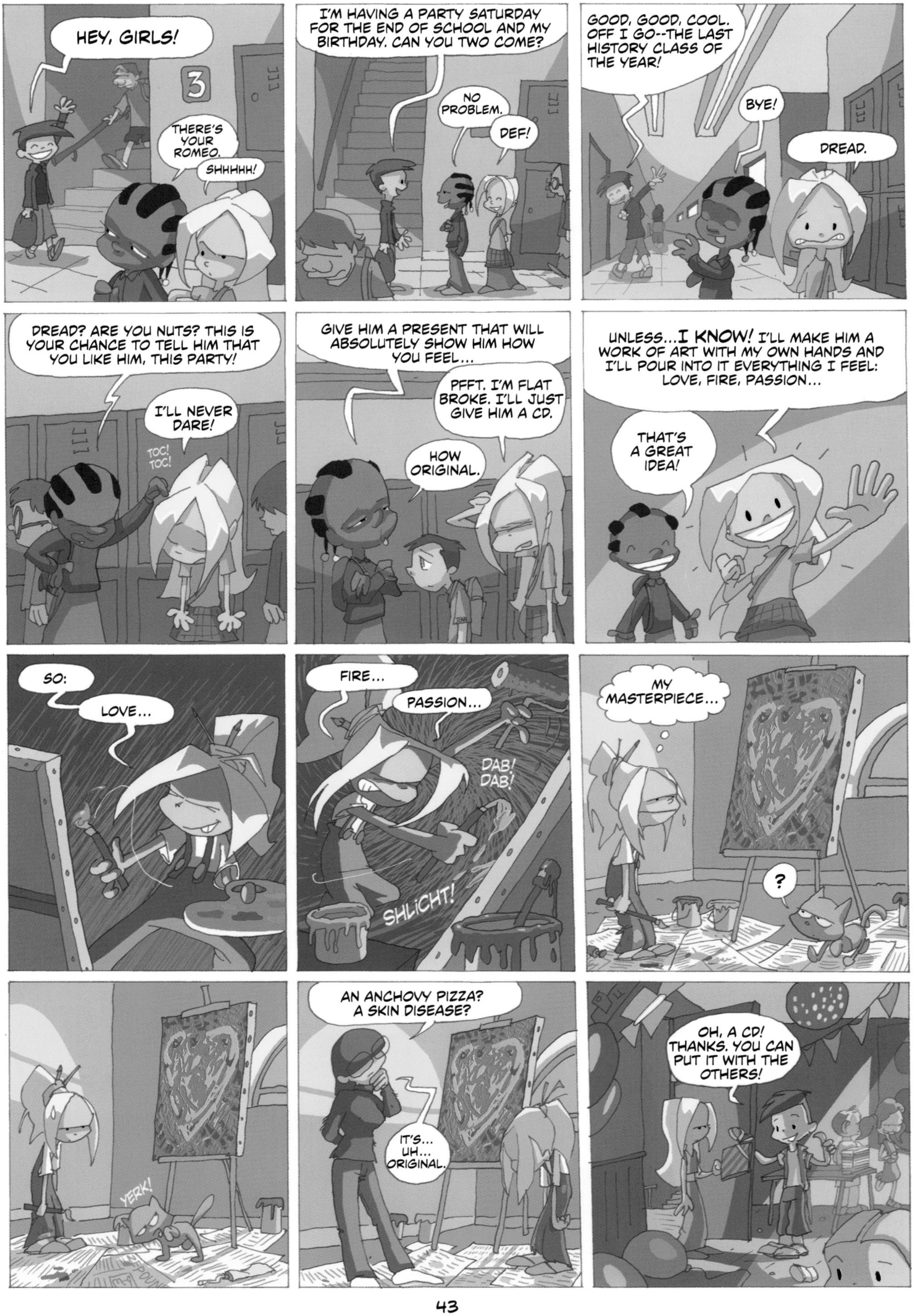
HEY, GIRLS!
3
THERE'S YOUR ROMEO.
SHHHHH!
I'M HAVING A PARTY SATURDAY FOR THE END OF SCHOOL AND MY BIRTHDAY. CAN YOU TWO COME?
NO PROBLEM.
DEF!
GOOD, GOOD, COOL. OFF I GO--THE LAST HISTORY CLASS OF THE YEAR!
BYE!
DREAD.
DREAD? ARE YOU NUTS? THIS IS YOUR CHANCE TO TELL HIM THAT YOU LIKE HIM, THIS PARTY!
I'LL NEVER DARE!
TOC! TOC!
GIVE HIM A PRESENT THAT WILL ABSOLUTELY SHOW HIM HOW YOU FEEL...
PFFT. I'M FLAT BROKE. I'LL JUST GIVE HIM A CD.
HOW ORIGINAL.
UNLESS...I KNOW! I'LL MAKE HIM A WORK OF ART WITH MY OWN HANDS AND I'LL POUR INTO IT EVERYTHING I FEEL: LOVE, FIRE, PASSION...
THAT'S A GREAT IDEA!
SO:
LOVE...
FIRE...
PASSION...
DAB! DAB!
SHLICHT!
MY MASTERPIECE...
?
YERK!
AN ANCHOVY PIZZA? A SKIN DISEASE?
IT'S... UH... ORIGINAL.
OH, A CD! THANKS. YOU CAN PUT IT WITH THE OTHERS!

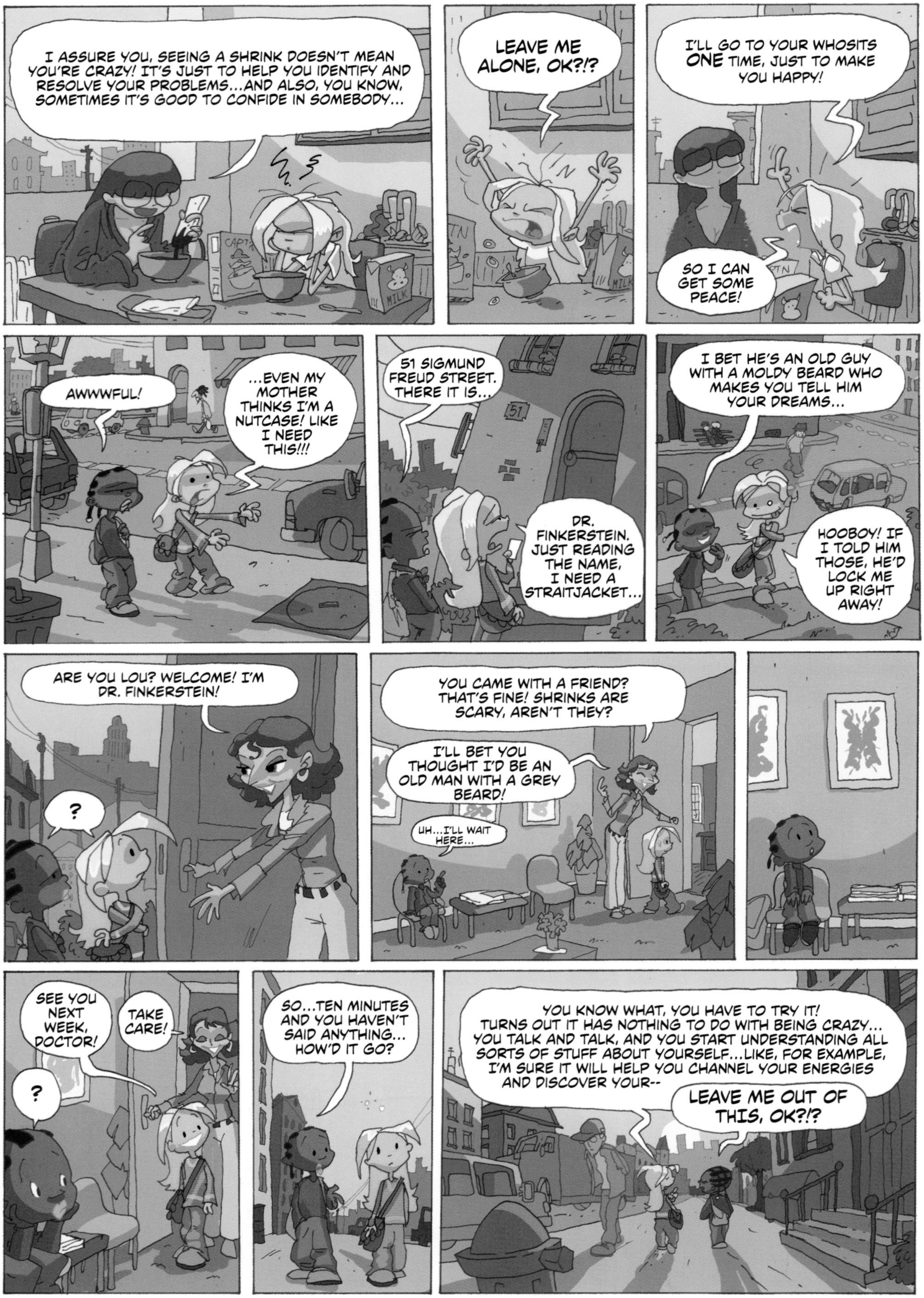
I ASSURE YOU, SEEING A SHRINK DOESN'T MEAN YOU'RE CRAZY! IT'S JUST TO HELP YOU IDENTIFY AND RESOLVE YOUR PROBLEMS...AND ALSO, YOU KNOW, SOMETIMES IT'S GOOD TO CONFIDE IN SOMEBODY...
LEAVE ME ALONE, OK?!?
I'LL GO TO YOUR WHOSITS ONE TIME, JUST TO MAKE YOU HAPPY!
SO I CAN GET SOME PEACE!
AWWWFUL!
...EVEN MY MOTHER THINKS I'M A NUTCASE! LIKE I NEED THIS!!!
51 SIGMUND FREUD STREET. THERE IT IS...
DR. FINKERSTEIN. JUST READING THE NAME, I NEED A STRAITJACKET...
I BET HE'S AN OLD GUY WITH A MOLDY BEARD WHO MAKES YOU TELL HIM YOUR DREAMS...
HOOBOY! IF I TOLD HIM THOSE, HE'D LOCK ME UP RIGHT AWAY!
ARE YOU LOU? WELCOME! I'M DR. FINKERSTEIN!
?
YOU CAME WITH A FRIEND? THAT'S FINE! SHRINKS ARE SCARY, AREN'T THEY?
I'LL BET YOU THOUGHT I'D BE AN OLD MAN WITH A GREY BEARD!
UH...I'LL WAIT HERE...
SEE YOU NEXT WEEK, DOCTOR!
TAKE CARE!
?
SO...TEN MINUTES AND YOU HAVEN'T SAID ANYTHING... HOW'D IT GO?
YOU KNOW WHAT, YOU HAVE TO TRY IT! TURNS OUT IT HAS NOTHING TO DO WITH BEING CRAZY... YOU TALK AND TALK, AND YOU START UNDERSTANDING ALL SORTS OF STUFF ABOUT YOURSELF...LIKE, FOR EXAMPLE, I'M SURE IT WILL HELP YOU CHANNEL YOUR ENERGIES AND DISCOVER YOUR--
LEAVE ME OUT OF THIS, OK?!?

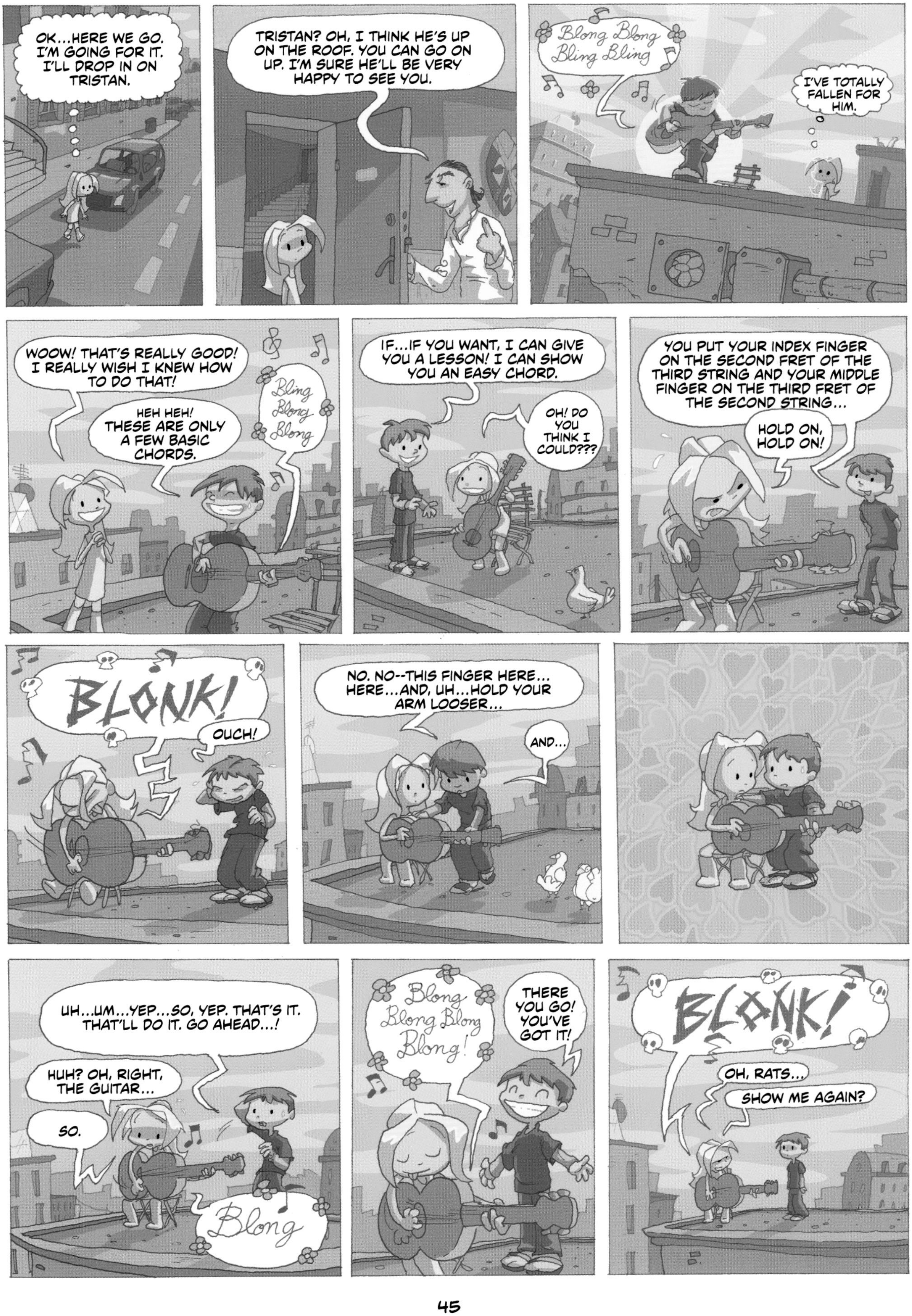
OK...HERE WE GO. I'M GOING FOR IT. I'LL DROP IN ON TRISTAN.
TRISTAN? OH, I THINK HE'S UP ON THE ROOF. YOU CAN GO ON UP. I'M SURE HE'LL BE VERY HAPPY TO SEE YOU.
Blong Blong Bling Bling
I'VE TOTALLY FALLEN FOR HIM.
WOOW! THAT'S REALLY GOOD! I REALLY WISH I KNEW HOW TO DO THAT!
HEH HEH! THESE ARE ONLY A FEW BASIC CHORDS.
Bling Blong Blong
IF...IF YOU WANT, I CAN GIVE YOU A LESSON! I CAN SHOW YOU AN EASY CHORD.
OH! DO YOU THINK I COULD???
YOU PUT YOUR INDEX FINGER ON THE SECOND FRET OF THE THIRD STRING AND YOUR MIDDLE FINGER ON THE THIRD FRET OF THE SECOND STRING...
HOLD ON, HOLD ON!
BLONK!
OUCH!
NO. NO--THIS FINGER HERE... HERE...AND, UH...HOLD YOUR ARM LOOSER...
AND...
UH...UM...YEP...SO, YEP. THAT'S IT. THAT'LL DO IT. GO AHEAD...!
HUH? OH, RIGHT, THE GUITAR...
SO.
Blong
Blong Blong Blong Blong!
THERE YOU GO! YOU'VE GOT IT!
BLONK!
OH, RATS...
SHOW ME AGAIN?

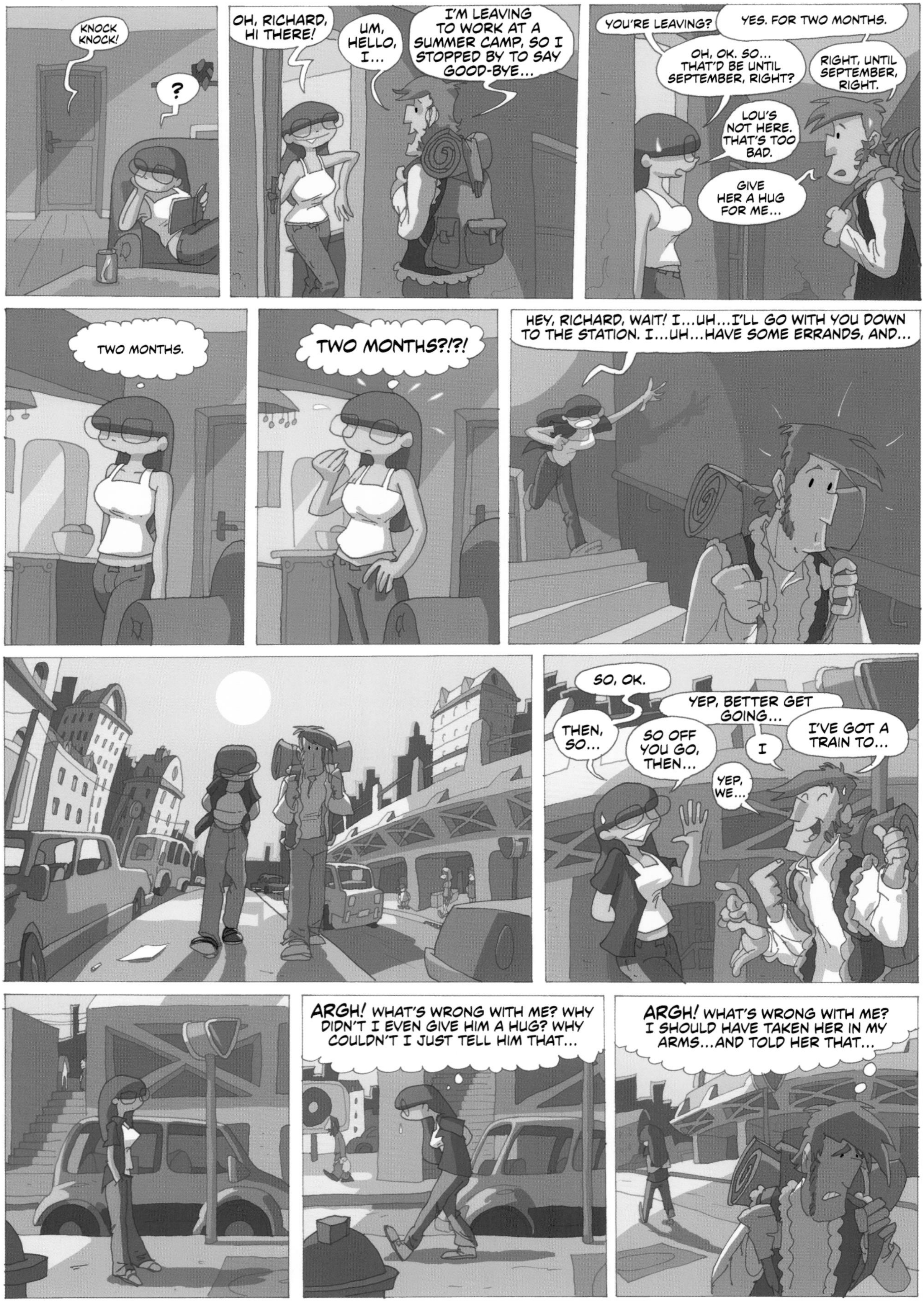
KNOCK KNOCK!
?
OH, RICHARD, HI THERE!
UM, HELLO, I...
I'M LEAVING TO WORK AT A SUMMER CAMP, SO I STOPPED BY TO SAY GOOD-BYE...
YOU'RE LEAVING?
YES. FOR TWO MONTHS.
OH, OK. SO... THAT'D BE UNTIL SEPTEMBER, RIGHT?
RIGHT, UNTIL SEPTEMBER, RIGHT.
LOU'S NOT HERE. THAT'S TOO BAD.
GIVE HER A HUG FOR ME...
TWO MONTHS.
TWO MONTHS?!?!
HEY, RICHARD, WAIT! I...UH...I'LL GO WITH YOU DOWN TO THE STATION. I...UH...HAVE SOME ERRANDS, AND...
SO, OK.
THEN, SO...
YEP, BETTER GET GOING...
SO OFF YOU GO, THEN...
I
I'VE GOT A TRAIN TO...
YEP, WE...
ARGH! WHAT'S WRONG WITH ME? WHY DIDN'T I EVEN GIVE HIM A HUG? WHY COULDN'T I JUST TELL HIM THAT...
ARGH! WHAT'S WRONG WITH ME? I SHOULD HAVE TAKEN HER IN MY ARMS...AND TOLD HER THAT...

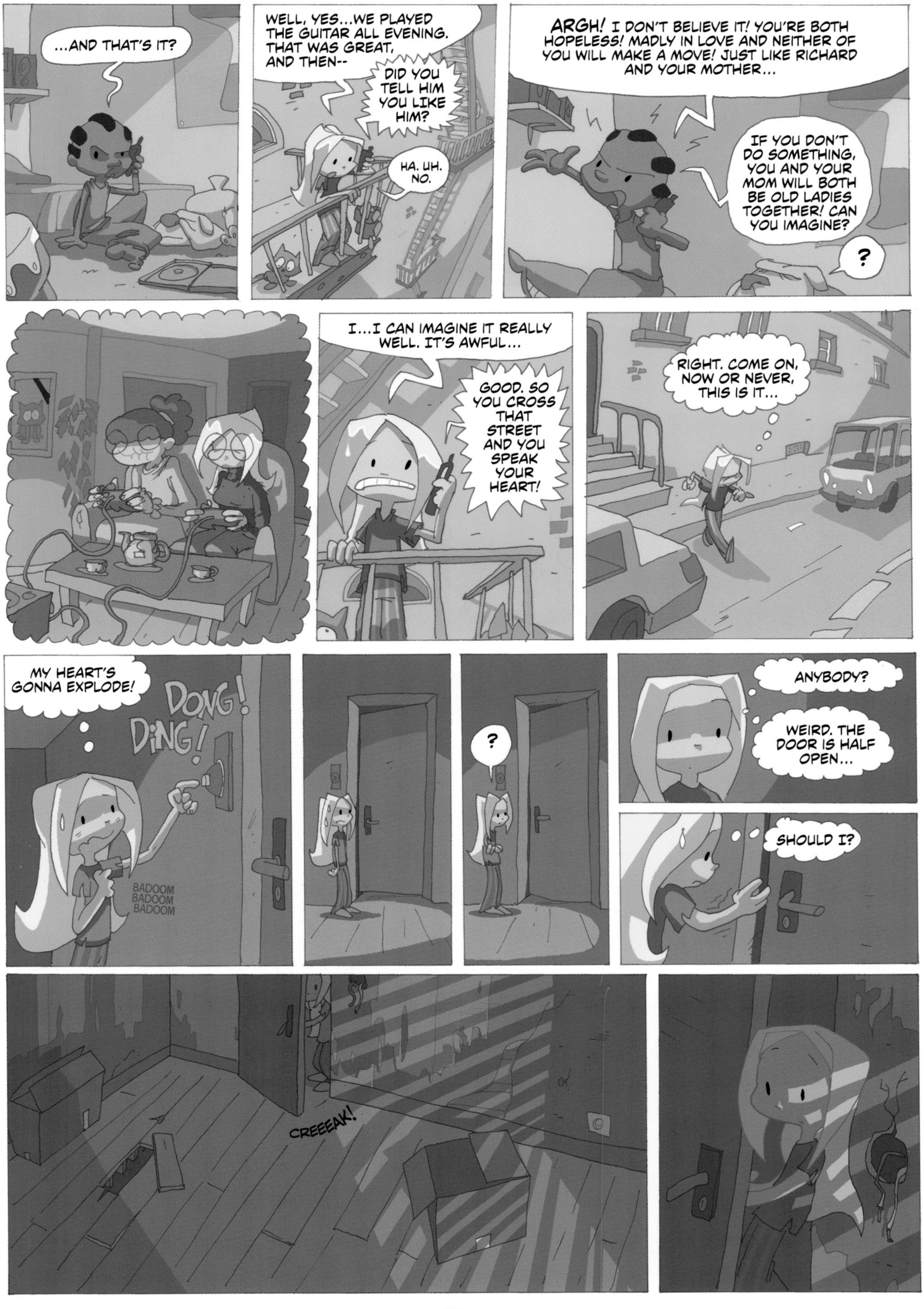
...AND THAT'S IT?
WELL, YES...WE PLAYED THE GUITAR ALL EVENING. THAT WAS GREAT, AND THEN--
DID YOU TELL HIM YOU LIKE HIM?
HA. UH. NO.
ARGH! I DON'T BELIEVE IT! YOU'RE BOTH HOPELESS! MADLY IN LOVE AND NEITHER OF YOU WILL MAKE A MOVE! JUST LIKE RICHARD AND YOUR MOTHER...
IF YOU DON'T DO SOMETHING, YOU AND YOUR MOM WILL BOTH BE OLD LADIES TOGETHER! CAN YOU IMAGINE?
?
I...I CAN IMAGINE IT REALLY WELL. IT'S AWFUL...
GOOD. SO YOU CROSS THAT STREET AND YOU SPEAK YOUR HEART!
RIGHT. COME ON, NOW OR NEVER, THIS IS IT...
MY HEART'S GONNA EXPLODE!
DING!
DONG!
BADOOM
BADOOM
BADOOM
?
ANYBODY?
WEIRD. THE DOOR IS HALF OPEN...
SHOULD I?
CREEEAK!

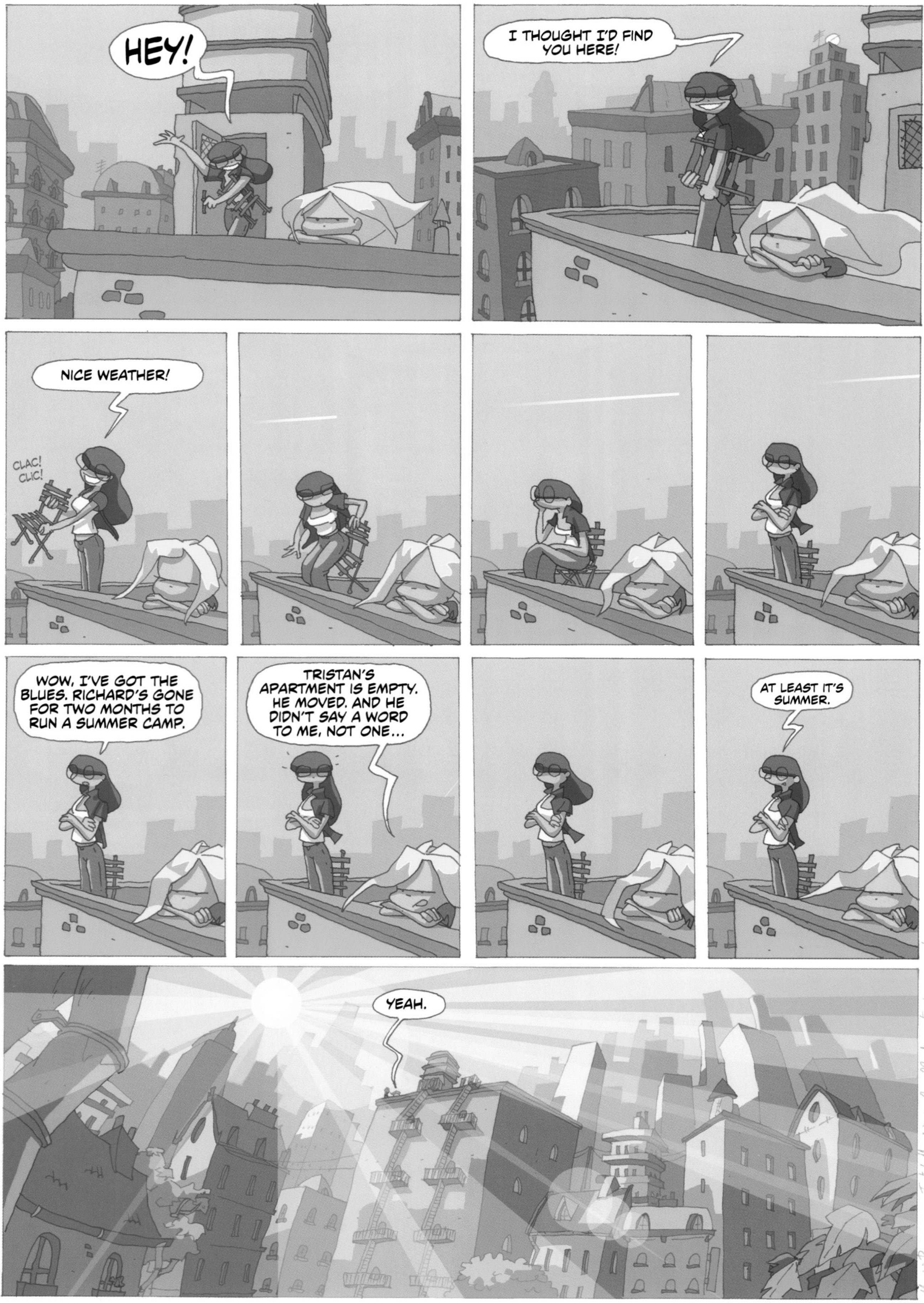
HEY!
I THOUGHT I'D FIND YOU HERE!
NICE WEATHER!
CLAC! CLIC!
WOW, I'VE GOT THE BLUES. RICHARD'S GONE FOR TWO MONTHS TO RUN A SUMMER CAMP.
TRISTAN'S APARTMENT IS EMPTY. HE MOVED. AND HE DIDN'T SAY A WORD TO ME, NOT ONE...
AT LEAST IT'S SUMMER.
YEAH.

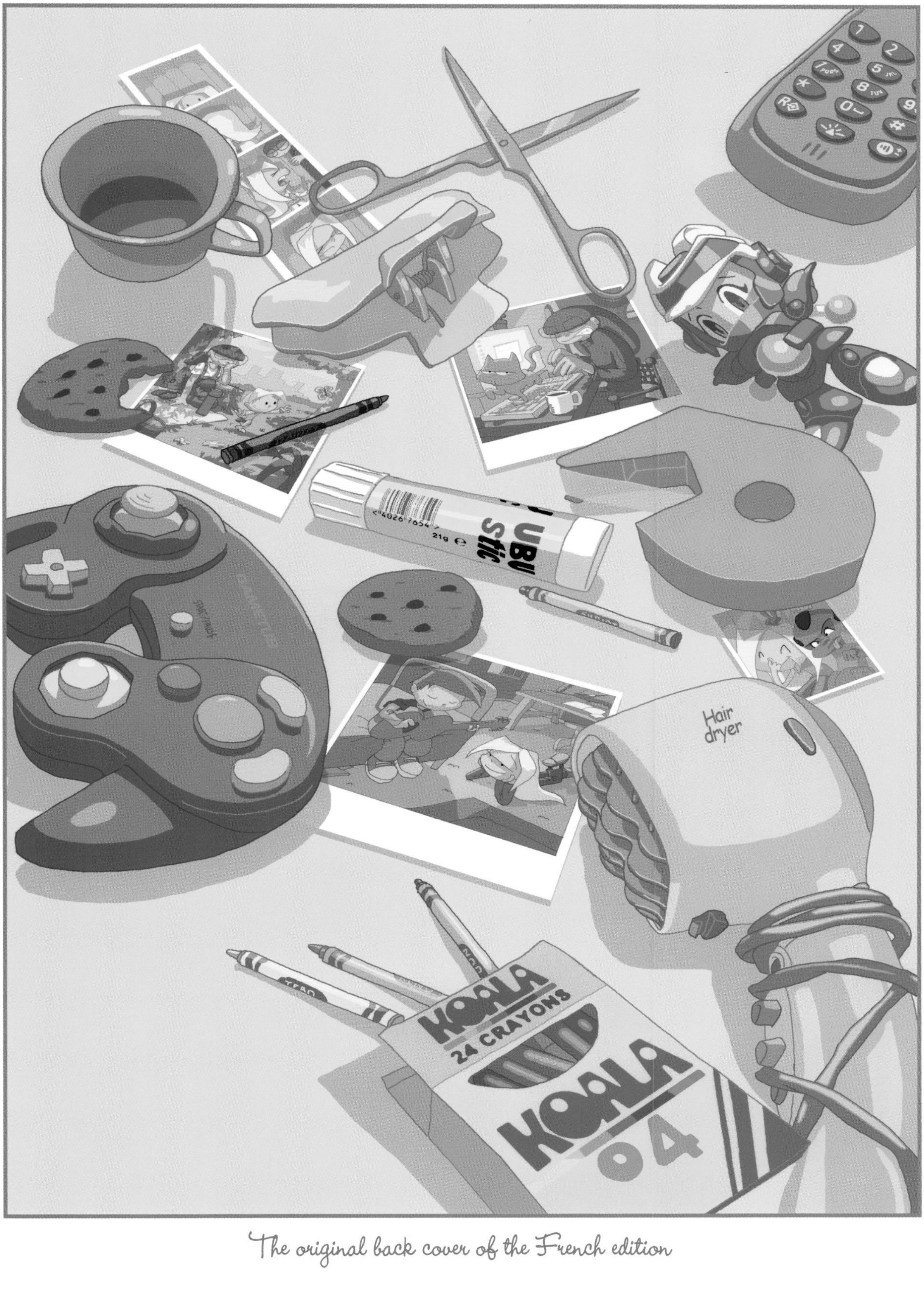
UBU
stic
21g
GAMETUB
Hair
dryer
KOALA
24 CRAYONS
KOALA
04

The original back cover of the French edition

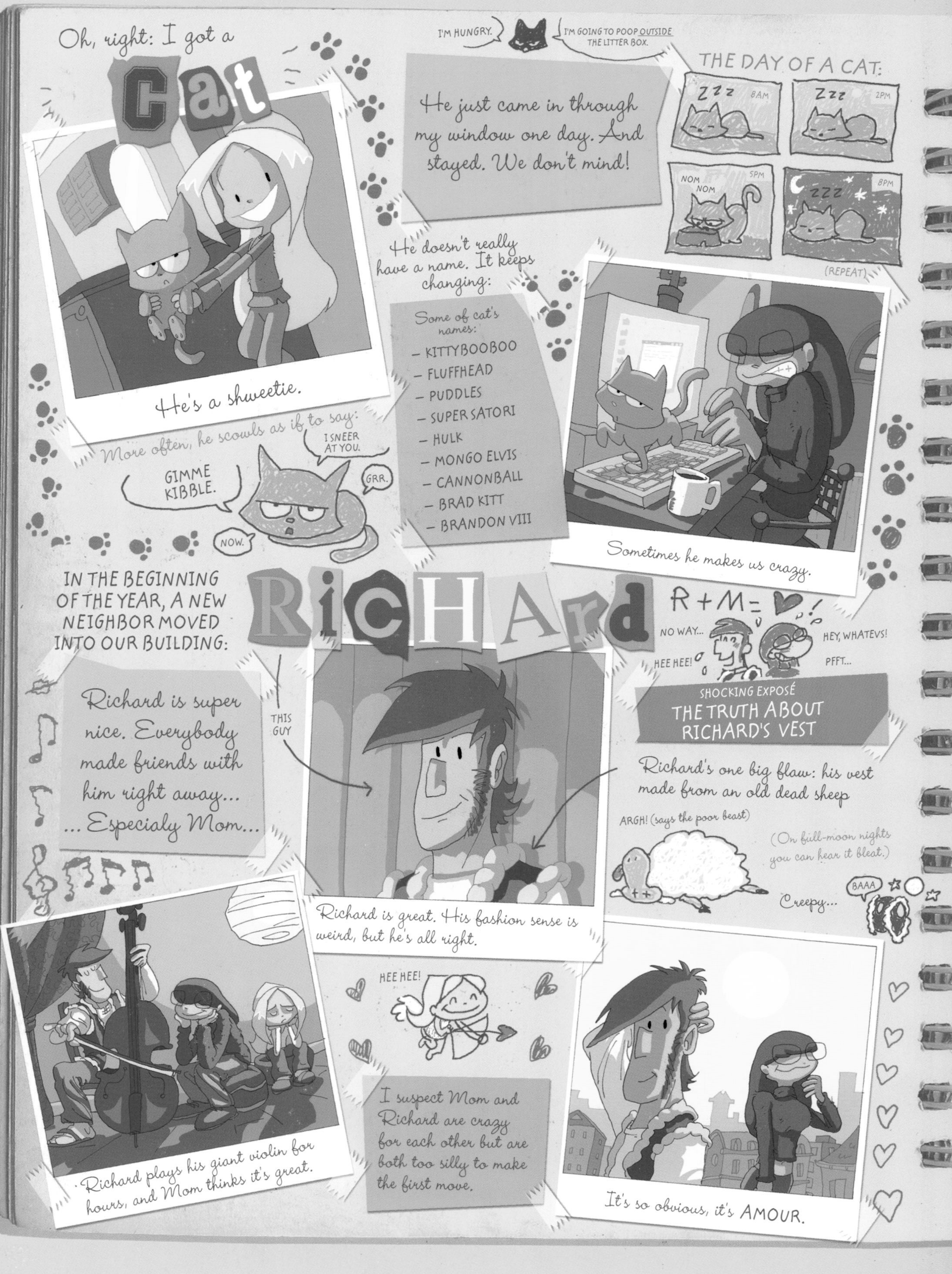

Oh, right: I got a
Cat
He's a shweetie.
I'M HUNGRY.
I'M GOING TO POOP OUTSIDE THE LITTER BOX.
He just came in through my window one day. And stayed. We don't mind!
THE DAY OF A CAT:
ZZZ 8AM
ZZZ 2PM
NOM NOM 5PM
ZZZ 8PM
(REPEAT)
More often, he scowls as if to say:
GIMME KIBBLE.
I SNEER AT YOU.
GRR.
NOW.
He doesn't really have a name. It keeps changing:
Some of cat's names:
– KITTYBOOBOO
– FLUFFHEAD
– PUDDLES
– SUPER SATORI
– HULK
– MONGO ELVIS
– CANNONBALL
– BRAD KITT
– BRANDON VIII
Sometimes he makes us crazy.
IN THE BEGINNING OF THE YEAR, A NEW NEIGHBOR MOVED INTO OUR BUILDING:
RiCHArd
R + M =
NO WAY...
HEY, WHATEVS!
HEE HEE!
PFFT...
Richard is super nice. Everybody made friends with him right away... ... Especialy Mom...
THIS GUY
SHOCKING EXPOSÉ
THE TRUTH ABOUT RICHARD'S VEST
Richard's one big flaw: his vest made from an old dead sheep
ARGH! (says the poor beast)
(On full-moon nights you can hear it bleat.)
BAAA
Creepy...
Richard is great. His fashion sense is weird, but he's all right.
Richard plays his giant violin for hours, and Mom thinks it's great.
HEE HEE!
I suspect Mom and Richard are crazy for each other but are both too silly to make the first move.
It's so obvious, it's AMOUR.